"So are you and God back on speaking terms?"

"We're working on it." Cam took some popcorn and munched for a few seconds. "I got together with my pastor this week."

Rachel wanted to shout *yes!* but forced herself to sit still. "How did that go?"

A slight smile lifted the corners of his mouth. "It'll take a while to rebuild our friendship, but we're both committed to that."

She nodded. "Sounds like you're on a good path, Cam. I'm happy for you."

"Thanks. It's taken me a while, but I think I'm ready for whatever God has in store for me in this next phase of life." The look in his eyes told her he wasn't only thinking about getting closer to God. He was talking about a relationship with her.

Her heartbeat quickened. Was she ready to take the next step with Cam?

There was no need to make any decisions tonight. She had time to see what would develop. But she realized her heart had already made up its mind....

Books by Carrie Turansky

Love Inspired

Along Came Love
Seeking His Love

CARRIE TURANSKY

and her husband, Scott, live in beautiful central New Jersey. They are blessed with five great kids, a lovely daughter-in-law and an adorable grandson. Carrie home schools her two youngest children, teaches women's Bible studies and enjoys reading, gardening and walking around the lake near their home. After her family lived in Kenya as missionaries for a year, Carrie missed Africa so much she decided to write a novel set there to relive her experiences. That novel sits on a shelf and will probably never be published, but it stirred her desire to tell stories that touch hearts with God's love. *Along Came Love* was Carrie's debut novel with Steeple Hill. She loves hearing from her readers. You may e-mail her at carrie@carrieturansky.com. You're also invited to visit her Web site at www.carrieturansky.com.

Seeking His Love
Carrie Turansky

Steeple Hill®

Published by Steeple Hill Books™

STEEPLE HILL BOOKS

Steeple Hill®

ISBN-13: 978-0-373-81507-4

SEEKING HIS LOVE

Copyright © 2010 by Carrie Turansky

"Blessed are they who keep His statutes and seek Him with all their heart."
—*Psalms* 119:2

To my friends Cathy Gohlke and Terri Gillespie for their love and encouragement on my writing journey.

Chapter One

Rachel Clark stepped into the dark auditorium of the old Fairhaven School, and a shiver of anticipation raced up her back. Cool air ushered a dusty smell toward her, teasing her nose. With only the dim glow of the exit signs to show her the path, she walked down the sloping aisle toward the stage.

The house lights came up. She blinked at the sudden brightness and took in the scene. Rows of padded folding seats in three sections filled the cavernous hall. Two carpeted aisles led to a large stage with a plush burgundy curtain.

Warmth and wonder tingled through her. "This is perfect." She turned and searched for Hannah Bodine.

The silver-haired curator of the local historical museum poked her head out from the sound booth at the back. Dressed in a flowing tropical-print blouse and coral capri pants, she stepped into the aisle. "Do you like it?"

"Yes, it's exactly what we're looking for." Rachel hurried forward and mounted the steps. Waltzing to the middle of the stage, she scanned the auditorium. "Do you know how many seats there are?"

"Let's see." Hannah strolled forward, counting the rows of burgundy chairs. "Looks like almost four hundred."

Rachel smiled and nodded. "That's a hundred more than we have now." With a larger house they could increase their ticket sales and income, something she and her small staff desperately needed if they were going to hold on to their jobs.

"I think this would be a good home for your group," Hannah added. "Why don't I take you to meet Cameron McKenna, and you can make arrangements to speak to everyone at the co-op meeting tonight."

"That would be great." Rachel ran her hand along the velvet curtain as she crossed the stage, memories of past performances making her smile. She descended the wooden steps and met her friend down in front.

"Thanks, Hannah. I was beginning to think we were going to be a homeless theater company." Rachel crossed her arms and rubbed away a chill at that thought.

"It works out well for all of us. The school district

is raising our rent." Hannah sighed and shook her head as she led the way up the aisle. "You'd think they'd be happy to receive any income from this old building. It sat empty for two years before we got together to rent it. We've made a lot of improvements, but if we want to hold on to it, we have to rent the remaining space."

Rachel nodded. It sounded like the Fairhaven Artists' Co-op needed her as much as she needed them. She blew out a deep breath and tried to relax her tense shoulders. This would work. It had to.

Finding the position as director of Northcoast Christian Youth Theater had been an amazing answer to prayer. She didn't want to think about disbanding and looking for another job. Returning to teaching wasn't an option, not after everything that had happened. She pushed those painful memories away and followed Hannah into the main hallway.

"That's Cam's frame shop." Hannah motioned toward the open door across the hall. "He handles all the finances for the co-op. He can give you the particulars about renting with us."

Rachel stepped forward, eager to meet him and discuss the details.

Hannah held out her hand to slow her down. "Cam might be a bit resistant to the idea. He's a little…" She bit her lip. "Well, I suppose I should let you make up your own mind. Just be patient with him, dear."

Rachel smiled and nodded, certain she'd have no trouble winning him over. Persuasion was her middle name. Her exasperated mother used to say she could sell a dozen umbrellas to a desert nomad with no trouble at all.

She entered the shop where framed prints, photos and original artwork lined the walls. Rows of mat and frame samples hung in a neat display on the back wall.

A tall man with broad shoulders and blond curly hair leaned over a workbench at the rear of the shop. He held a pair of needle-nose pliers in his hand. The muscles on his forearm rippled as he twisted a sturdy wire to create a hanger across the back of a large frame lying facedown on the workbench. He looked up, and his piercing blue gaze connected with hers.

A shiver of awareness traveled through her. She straightened and returned his steady gaze. He looked about thirty-five, with a strong chin and Roman nose. No doubt he'd be handsome if he didn't wear such a scowl.

"Good morning, Cam." Hannah crossed to the workbench and Rachel followed.

"Morning." He nodded to Hannah.

"This is Rachel Clark. She's interested in renting space with us."

His scowl softened, and he lifted his golden brows. "What kind of artwork do you do?"

"I'm the director of a theater group. We're interested in renting the auditorium, two classrooms and an office."

"That's a lot of space." He laid aside the pliers. "Is this a new group, or are you already established?"

"We're about four years old." Uneasiness prickled through her. She'd only been working as the director since the beginning of March, a little more than two months. But she had six years of teaching high school drama and three summers with N.C.Y.T. as the assistant director. So she wasn't stretching the truth too far when she included herself in that four-year history.

He looked her over more carefully. "Where are you meeting now?"

"We use Grace Community Church in North Bellingham, but they're opening a preschool, so we need to be out by the end of May."

Recognition flickered in his eyes. "Is Sheldon James the pastor there?"

"Yes. Do you know him?"

"We're old friends."

"He and the church have been very supportive."

"Sheldon is a good man." He wiped his hand on a cloth. "So what kind of shows do you do?"

"They're all musicals. Our last two were *Annie* and *Oklahoma*. This summer we're doing *Anne of Green Gables*."

He continued to appraise her with his sharp gaze. "What do you call yourselves?"

She hesitated a split second, sending off a silent prayer. "Northcoast Christian Youth Theater."

His eyes widened, and a stormy expression broke over his face. "*Youth?* As in *children?*"

"Yes. Our students are ten to eighteen. We hold afterschool drama classes September to May, and morning drama camps in the summer, along with afternoon and evening rehearsals for our musicals."

He gave a swift shake of his head. "That would never work here."

A shot of panic skittered along her nerves. "But you have the space. And, from what Hannah said, you need to rent it."

He sent Hannah a disapproving glance, then turned back to Rachel. "We're serious artists. Our shops are filled with expensive pieces. We can't have kids running all over the building."

Heat flashed into Rachel's face. "I can assure you my students are well supervised."

"Sorry. I can't take that risk."

Rachel pulled in a calming breath. "I'm sure when you learn more about our program, you'll see how valuable we are to the community."

"It may be a good program, but it would be a bad idea to bring it here."

Hannah laid her hand on the workbench. "Cam,

my granddaughter attends the summer camp and has been in two shows. I've seen the performances. They're a wonderful group of kids."

Rachel sent Hannah a grateful smile, then turned to Cam. "Renting to us would bring in more customers."

He huffed. "The kids are going to buy artwork?"

"No, but their parents bring them to classes and rehearsals, and that would be the perfect opportunity for them to visit the shops and galleries. Plus you'd be connecting with all the friends and family who attend our performances. More than half our shows sold out last year. We've built a great reputation." Her enthusiasm mounted as she continued. "Maybe we could hold a special opening-night reception and invite everyone to come early and tour the building."

"I still don't see how you can mix a children's theater group with professional artists."

"Then let me come to the meeting tonight and make my presentation. I'm sure you'll want to move ahead when you see how this can benefit everyone." She held her breath. *Lord, please, please let him agree.*

Crossing his arms, he studied her for a few more nerve-racking seconds.

She maintained eye contact, though she could feel her left eyelid begin to twitch.

Finally, he blew out a deep breath. "All right. You can come. But I'm not promising anything."

Triumph pulsed through her, and she could barely keep from pumping her fist in the air and shouting, "Yes!"

Cam paced across the shop to the window. Leaning on the counter covering the radiator, he watched Rachel Clark stride toward the parking lot, her dark brown hair swishing against her shoulders. She had spunk and determination. He could see it in the tilt of his chin and hear it in her voice. And those big brown eyes of hers could melt any guy's heart.

But he couldn't let that get to him. No way would he let a pack of wild kids take over the building and jeopardize his business. Hopefully the rest of his friends in the co-op would agree. But he suspected Rachel would spin her story in a way that made him look like a hard-hearted jerk if he said no to her. Well, that couldn't be helped. He had to do what was best for the co-op, even if he ended up looking like the bad guy.

Kids were okay. He could tolerate them, but he tried to avoid them most of the time.

It had taken four years to distance himself from the painful experiences that had altered his life. He didn't want to rub those wounds raw again. For his own sanity, he couldn't.

Focusing out the window once more, he watched

Rachel climb into a white Toyota that looked like it had seen too many miles down the freeway. She glanced back at the building, and even at a distance he could see the longing on her face.

He clamped his jaw against his softening resolve and stepped back from the window. He wasn't going to destroy his dreams just for a pair of pretty brown eyes.

He'd be voting against Rachel Clark tonight, and if he had his way, so would everyone else.

Chapter Two

Cam grabbed photographer Ross Peterson by the elbow the second he walked through the door and steered him toward the front corner of Lilly Wong's gallery. The co-op meeting would start as soon as Hannah and Rachel arrived. He'd have to make this fast.

Cam scanned the room to be sure no one was looking, then he tugged Ross behind a display partition.

Ross pushed his black-framed glasses up his thin nose and sent Cam a quizzical look. "What's going on?"

"I need to fill you in before the meeting starts."

"Okay, but could you let go of me? You're cutting off my circulation."

"Oh. Sorry." Cam dropped Ross's arm and took a quick glance over his shoulder. "There's a woman coming tonight to talk to us about renting some space."

"So, that's good, isn't it?"

"No! It's definitely *not* good. We don't want to rent to her."

"But we've got to fill the building, or we'll never get out of the red."

"She wants to bring in a children's theater group." A movement in the hallway caught Cam's attention. "There she is," he whispered.

Rachel and Hannah walked in together, looking like old friends. Hannah laughed at something Rachel said, then crossed the room and introduced her to Lilly and Melanie Howard, two of the other co-op artists.

Ross fixed his gaze on Rachel, and his expression grew mellow. "Wow. Where's my camera when I need it?"

Cam grabbed his friend's shoulder. "Ross, pay attention! She wants to rent about a third of the building."

"That would be great." Ross watched her with a dumbstruck smile on his face.

"Are you kidding? We're talking about herds of kids swarming all over the place. We've got to get rid of her."

Ross pulled back and squinted at him. "There is something seriously wrong with you."

"Why? Because I don't want to turn our building into a day care center?"

"No, because we've got to rent that space, and we don't have any other prospects. I'm sure we can work something out."

"But she's—"

Melanie looked around the end of the partition. "Oh, there you are. Everyone's here. We should get started."

"Be right there." Cam shot a warning look at Ross. "Don't let her sentimental stories sway you. This is a dangerous idea."

Amusement lit Ross's eyes, and he patted Cam on the back. "Come on. Let's grab some coffee and a few of Lilly's brownies. Maybe the caffeine jolt will get your brain back on track."

Cam scoffed but followed Ross toward the coffeepot. He filled a tall ceramic mug with steaming brew, then added plenty of cream and sugar. Maybe he was overreacting a little, but how else could he convince his friend that renting to Rachel Clark would spell disaster for the co-op?

He took a sip and glanced across the top of his mug. Rachel sure didn't fit his image of a drama director. No flamboyant colors or avant-garde style. Just simple black pants that showed off her long slim legs and a soft blue sweater that accentuated her feminine figure.

He pulled his gaze away and took a big gulp of hot

coffee. *Maintain your focus. It doesn't matter that she's attractive.* His first concern had to be protecting the interests of the co-op. That was his priority, not helping Rachel Clark.

"Okay. Let's all take a seat and get started." Cam motioned toward the large rectangular table in the center of Lilly's gallery. She had cleared away her paintings so they could gather around the table for their meeting. Cam settled in a leather desk chair at one end, and Ross sat on his right. Melanie took the chair on his left, and Lilly sat beside Melanie.

Hannah motioned for Rachel to sit at the end of the table opposite Cam, and then she took the last open seat next to her.

Cam grimaced. He didn't relish the idea of facing Rachel all evening, but there was nothing he could do about it now. Frowning, he opened a file and shuffled a stack of papers. Maybe he would let her give her spiel first and get it over with. Then they could get on to more important business and hopefully get something done tonight.

Cam cleared his throat and gazed down the length of the table at Rachel. "All right. We have several items on the agenda, but first let's hear from Rachel Clark."

Rachel blinked and sucked in a quick breath. No intro? No explanation? She'd at least hoped for a few minutes to observe the group before she began her presentation. It looked like she'd just have to dive in and hope the current didn't wash her away.

Drawing on her theatrical training, she stood and put on a confident smile. "Thank you. I appreciate the opportunity to meet with you tonight. As Mr. McKenna said, my name is Rachel Clark. I'm the director of Northcoast Christian Youth Theater, and we're looking for a new location."

As an actress, Rachel had been trained to observe and interpret body language, and this was the perfect time to put those skills to work.

Hannah smiled, approval obvious in her soft gray eyes. Lilly watched with an open, pleasant expression, her head tipped thoughtfully to the left, her chin-length black hair falling against her cheek. Melanie, on the other hand, sent out a negative vibe with a calculating gaze that flicked back and forth from Cam to Rachel. Ross tapped a pen quietly on his knee, a slight smile on his lips as he gazed at Rachel through his dark-rimmed glasses. Cam sat back, his mouth set in a firm line, daring her to change his mind.

She pulled in a deep breath and made eye contact with each person around the table. Time to state the facts and pray for grace. "There are three reasons why we would be an excellent group to share your facility.

"Number one, we can dramatically increase your exposure to the community. The parents of our students often drive a distance to bring their children to classes, rehearsals and performances. And they usually wait in the building until their children are finished. Those parents would be potential new customers."

Interest lit the faces around the table.

"Number two, we want to rent the auditorium, two classrooms and an office. That will greatly increase your income and give you more funds for improvements. Or you could use the extra money to decrease the amount of rent each of you is paying."

Hannah nodded and smiled, exchanging a look with Lilly.

"Number three, we provide an outstanding program that benefits youth and families and strengthens the community. And a stronger community benefits everyone.

"At N.C.Y.T. we teach more than music and drama skills," she continued. "We place a high priority on developing character and teaching values like commitment, discipline and confidence. Your association with us will enhance your reputation and build even stronger bridges to the community."

Ross leaned forward, his expression warm and encouraging.

Her hopes rose. At least she seemed to have found a few advocates among the group.

"As leaders, we seek to be role models for our students so they can see how to live out their faith and values in everyday life. We believe N.C.Y.T. is a unique program that's making a positive impact."

Cam cocked his brows at a skeptical angle. "Those are noble goals, but I don't see how filling our building with kids is going to have a very *positive* impact on us."

Melanie nodded, her sour expression reflecting Cam's. "How many kids are we talking about?"

"We have forty to fifty students in our after-school and summer-camp programs and about thirty involved in the musicals." Rachel's stomach tightened as she watched their response to the numbers.

"I know that sounds like a large group, but let me give you an example of the kind of kids there are in our program. Last July a crisis hit the N.C.Y.T. family. Jordan Webster's sister, Hope, was born with a serious heart defect, and she needed an expensive surgery. Medical insurance covered only a portion of the expenses.

"When the kids heard about it, they wanted to help. They planned two extra performances of our summer musical. Then they contacted the newspaper, promoted it all over the area and raised more than $8,000 to help the Websters. Little Hope had the surgery and she's doing well. And those kids will never forget how great it feels to be a part of saving someone's life."

Hannah nodded, her eyes shining. "I attended one of those performances."

"I remember reading about it in the paper," Lilly added. "Quite a contrast to most of the stories you read about kids these days."

"They sound like a great group," Ross added.

Rachel nodded. "We're a caring community, and those are the kind of neighbors you'll have if you'll partner with us and provide a new location for N.C.Y.T."

Cam looked away and cleared his throat. "Okay. We have the information we need to discuss this among ourselves. Would you mind stepping out in the hall?"

His dismissal caught her by surprise, but she quickly recovered. "Of course." She picked up her purse and headed toward the door.

Had she convinced them? Would they allow her to rent the space she needed? Uncertainty nibbled away at her confidence as she walked out of the room. Perhaps her persuasive power hadn't done the trick this time, at least it didn't seem to have any affect on someone as hard-hearted as Cameron McKenna.

Chapter Three

Rachel strode to the drinking fountain and took a long sip of cool water. It quenched her thirst, but did little to ease her tension. She glanced at her watch and back at the closed door of Lilly's gallery. What was taking so long? She'd been out in the hall for at least fifteen minutes.

She blew out a deep breath and looked at the colorful banners overhead. They reminded her of hand-painted Chinese kites. Each one depicted a different Washington wildflower or bird. They added a touch of whimsy, softening the old, school atmosphere and giving the building the feeling of an artists' village.

She slipped down the hall and tiptoed up to the door. Leaning closer, she tried to make sense of the muffled conversation. The sound of footsteps approached. She quickly stepped back and smoothed down her hair.

The door opened. Hannah looked out and sent her a quick wink and a smile. "Come in and join us."

"Thanks." Rachel returned to her seat and looked across at Cam. A frown creased his forehead as he focused on his yellow legal pad.

"We're sorry we kept you waiting so long," Hannah said as she settled in her chair. "We needed to iron out a few details." The older woman's glance flashed to Cam. "We've agreed to lease you the space you asked for."

Relief rushed through Rachel. "Thank you. I'm sure it will be a good arrangement for all of us."

"We want to make certain of that." Cam lifted his gaze to meet hers. "The first six months will be a trial period. If things work out, we'll extend the lease. But if the kids cause problems, or the schedule is too intrusive, you'll have to leave at the end of the year."

Rachel swallowed. Was there room to negotiate a longer lease? A search of Cam's stern expression told her this was the only offer she would receive.

"I understand, and I assure you we'll do our best to be good neighbors."

Cam's only reply was a brief nod, then he moved on to discuss a landscaping project for the property and asked for a volunteer to contact garden centers for donations.

Rachel sat up straighter. She didn't know much about plants, but she wouldn't mind making a few calls. "I could work on that. There's a plant nursery just down the road from where I'm staying."

Ross nodded at Cam, apparently pleased by her offer.

Cam looked at her over the top of his reading glasses. "Do you have a connection there?"

"No, but they might be willing to help. What kind of plants are you looking for?"

Cam consulted his pad and reeled off a list. Rachel took notes as fast as she could, abbreviating some of the names and praying she'd remember what she meant.

Lilly smiled and slid a piece of paper across the table. "A friend who's a landscape architect did the design for us. He arranged for a donation of all the trees. The plants on Cam's list are bushes and perennial flowers."

Rachel nodded. "I'll contact the nursery right away."

"That would be wonderful." Hannah smiled, looking like a happy mother who had settled a disagreement between her children.

Melanie cleared her throat. "I could make a few calls. My uncle works as a city planner for Bellingham. I'm sure he has connections with several nurseries."

Rachel studied the woman who sat next to Cam. She looked a bit older than Rachel, probably in her mid-thirties. Though she had striking blue-green eyes, her large mouth and longish nose dominated her face. She wore her dark blond hair in a casual upswept style with a few tendrils hanging loose around her face. With a lift of her penciled brows, Melanie gazed back at Rachel, telegraphing a message that seemed to say, *"You had better watch yourself. You're not one of us yet."*

Cam made a note on his pad. "Okay. Why don't you both work on it and get back to us."

"Sounds good to me." Rachel was ready for the challenge and not about to be outdone. She'd find someone to donate those plants and prove she was just as capable as Melanie Howard, or anyone else.

Cam strolled out the door of Lilly's gallery after the co-op meeting. The group's conversation faded until all he heard was his footsteps on the tile floor. He returned to the frame shop, unlocked the door and flipped on the lights.

His shoulders sagged as he crossed the room and laid his pad, glasses and pen on the workbench. It was done. Rachel Clark and her kids were coming, and there was nothing he could do about it.

With a shake of his head, he grabbed the stack of orders from the shelf behind him and squinted at the clock. It was after nine. He should go home and get some rest. But that would be tough with the conflicting thoughts churning through his mind. Maybe if he worked for an hour or two he could clear his head and burn off some extra energy.

"Mr. McKenna?"

He looked up. "Yes?"

Rachel Clark stood in the doorway and sent him a tentative smile. "I wanted to thank you. I'm grateful we were able to work things out."

He frowned and looked away. "I don't know why you're thanking me. I'm the one who insisted on the trial period."

"Oh…. Well, I'm sure in a few weeks we'll have our program up and running, and you'll see this arrangement is going to be wonderful for everyone."

He studied her and rubbed his jaw. "Are you always this…upbeat?"

She blinked, looking confused. "Well, I guess I am a cup-half-full kind of person. I don't see any reason to be all gloomy and pessimistic."

He stiffened. "Is that what you think I am?" He hadn't intended to sound so gruff, but her perky attitude was getting to him.

"No, I didn't mean you specifically. I just—"

"Look, Ms. Bright Eyes. I don't care what you think of me. What matters is keeping the co-op afloat. If you and your kids fit in, fine. I won't give you any trouble. But if our building turns into an indoor playground—"

She glared at him. "You really are a piece of work, you know that?"

His jaw dropped, and the air whooshed out of his lungs as if she'd punched him.

She strode across the room and faced him from the other side of the workbench. "You know nothing about me or my kids. But you've already made up your mind I'm some kind of con artist, and my kids are a rowdy bunch of juvenile delinquents."

Cam lifted his hand. "Whoa. Hold on. I never—"

"No, *you* hold on. I came here tonight with good intentions. I'm not trying to pull anything over on you. Our group needs a new home, and this building is perfect. But I also believe this is a good arrangement for you and the co-op, or I wouldn't have come."

"Is that right?" He hoped he could take a little wind out of her billowing sails with his calm tone.

But her dark eyes flashed. "Yes, it is. So I wish you'd stop acting like I'm trying to trick you into something you'll regret."

Cam lifted both hands this time. "Okay. I hear you. You don't have to get upset."

She drew herself up. "I'm not upset." But she quickly deflated, and her fiery expression melted. "I'm sorry. I just hate it when I feel misjudged. That's a real hot button for me."

"I never would've guessed." He suppressed a smile and took a seat on his stool.

"Well, don't you think everyone deserves a fair

hearing?" She leaned on the workbench. "Shouldn't people have a chance to prove their innocence and explain their motives?"

He studied her, trying to discern where all this was coming from. She certainly seemed to have a strong sense of justice, especially where her intentions were concerned. "I'm all for giving everyone a chance to prove themselves. That's the reason behind the trial period, but you need to understand something. These people are my friends, not just my business partners. They've invested everything they have in their galleries, and most of them are hanging on by their teeth, hoping to make enough to pay the bills and hold on to their space. I need to watch out for them."

She nodded slowly, looking as though his words had finally sunk in. "How long have you all been working together?"

"About a year and half—not long enough to make much of a name for ourselves."

She sat on the stool in front of the workbench. "I'm sure it's a challenge to draw people in when you're not in the center of the historic district like most of the other galleries and shops."

"That's why we want to spruce up the building and add new landscaping and a better sign."

"Those are good ideas." She tucked a strand of dark brown hair behind her ear. "How about getting involved in craft fairs and community events? Or maybe you could offer some classes or hold an art show." Her eyes lit up as she continued, "Do you have a promotional brochure? How about a Web site? The Internet is a great way to reach people, and it's very cost-effective."

"You're just a fountain of ideas," he said, trying to resist the softening he felt toward her.

She shrugged, and her smile returned. "Promotion is part of my job. I enjoy it. Hannah gave me a tour of the galleries earlier. I'm excited about teaming up with you. I promise I'll do whatever I can to help get the word out."

This conversation was getting a little too cozy for him. He slid off the stool and stood. "Sure. That would be fine."

She seemed to pick up his silent message and pushed back from the workbench. "Well, it's getting late. I better go."

He glanced out his window at the dark parking lot. She might be the enemy, but he wasn't about to send her out there all alone. "I'll walk you out."

Her eyes glowed, and she sent him a grateful smile. "Thanks."

He grabbed his jacket and stuffed his cell phone in his pocket. He hoped he wasn't giving her the wrong idea. All he had in mind was making sure she was safe. He wasn't interested in anything else.

An occasional late-night walk to the car was all he planned to offer. And even that was a huge step for him.

Fresh, rain-washed air cooled Rachel's face as she stepped out the front door of the old school-turned-Arts-Center. She released a deep breath, letting go of the tension that had built through the evening. The aroma of lilacs and freshly mowed grass drifted past. She'd always loved those special springtime scents.

She glanced across at Cam as he fell in step beside her. His offer to walk her to her car had been a pleasant surprise. It seemed he hid some gentlemanly qualities under that brusque exterior after all.

Thinking back over the evening, she regretted the way she'd spouted off at him earlier. She'd been surprised by the way he took it all in stride.

Bright moonlight threw shadows across the sidewalk and highlighted the strong features of Cam's face. He slowed and looked to the right. "This is the area we want to landscape. We'll put flowers and shrubs in beds along the front of the building and lay sod over the rest." A faint smile lifted his mouth. "Maybe we should have our own outdoor art festival. There'd be plenty of room for it."

Rachel surveyed the weedy area, imagining the landscaping he'd described. "Sounds like a good idea." As she stepped off the curb, she glanced across the parking lot. A forest-green SUV sat under the central light near her white Toyota. Was that Cam's car? Then something else caught her attention. In the corner of the parking lot, a dark sedan sat in the shadows under the trees. A cigarette glowed behind the driver's side window for a second then disappeared.

Rachel pulled in a sharp breath, and her steps stalled.

Cam slowed next to her. "What's wrong?"

"There's someone in that car over there." She lifted her chin toward the car in the corner, trying not to be too obvious. The cigarette glowed again, and chilling memories came flooding back. Fear rose like a constricting band around her chest. She fought to pull in her next breath. This couldn't be happening again. *Please, God, not here. Not now.*

"It's probably just some guy who had a fight with his wife and needs a place to cool off." Though his tone was light, she saw him glance cautiously at the dark sedan as they approached her car.

She could feel Cam's steady gaze resting on her as she pulled her keys from her purse and sorted through them. Her hands shook. She clamped her teeth together, fighting the feeling of dread flowing through her. Now she not only had to worry about the man in the car, she had to try and hide her reaction from Cam. Explaining wasn't an option, not if she wanted to hold on to her job and new location.

A sudden wind whipped across the parking lot, sending bits of trash and dried leaves swirling around her. She brushed a strand of hair from her eyes and darted one more glance at the sedan. Was Cam right? Was this just a frightening coincidence?

She thought Fairhaven would be a safe place where she could start over and build a new life for herself— far away from the problems she'd experienced in Seattle.

But maybe she hadn't traveled far enough after all.

Chapter Four

The tantalizing aroma of fresh-brewed coffee floated by Cam's nose. He sniffed and looked up from cleaning the glass on his latest framing project.

Ross crossed the shop carrying two tall disposable cups. "One cream, two sugars." He held out a cup to Cam.

"Thanks. I owe you." He took a sip and scalded his tongue.

"You certainly do."

"What's that supposed to mean?"

His friend looked at him over the top of his glasses. "I saved your hide at the meeting last night, and you know it. If it weren't for me you would've totally alienated everyone."

Cam pulled off the plastic lid and blew across the top of the coffee. "Not everyone. Melanie agreed with me."

Ross huffed out a laugh. "That doesn't count. We

both know she'd agree to put in a tattoo parlor if you wanted it, and we know why." He wiggled his dark eyebrows and grinned like a Cheshire cat.

"I wish you'd leave it alone." Cam scowled at Ross. He usually ignored those jabs, but he was not in the mood today.

"Okay." Ross lifted his hand. "I won't mention it again."

Right. Cam would believe that when it happened. Ross loved to give him a hard time about Melanie's not-so-subtle hints that she'd like to be more than friends. But he also brought him coffee most mornings, shared take out pizza at least once a week, and wasn't put off by his moods. He supposed he could take a little ribbing from a friend like that.

Cam picked up a soft cloth and wiped a speck of dust from the corner of the frame. "I still can't believe we're going to be sharing our building with a kids' theater company. I'll probably have to invest in soundproofing and up my liability insurance."

"Come on, Cam. It won't be so bad. Maybe it'll bring some life into this place."

"Yeah. Life. Just what we need." He shook his head and took another gulp of coffee.

"It's a done deal. So you might as well…" Ross leaned left, looking past Cam's shoulder. A smile broke over his face. "Well, look who's here."

Cam turned and glanced out the window. A shiny black truck with the back full of boxes and furniture pulled into the loading zone out front. The driver's side door opened, and Rachel Clark hopped out.

His stomach tightened, and coffee-laced acid rose and burned his throat.

She must've known they were in a tough spot, and they'd have to say yes to her proposal. She'd probably already packed before the meeting last night.

Rachel walked around behind the truck and lowered the tailgate. Placing her hands on her hips, she studied the jumbled load for a second before she reached for the first box.

Ross set his coffee on Cam's desk. "Looks like she needs some help, and I'm just the man for the job." He walked to the doorway and turned back to Cam. "You coming?"

Cam frowned as he watched Rachel lift a large box. Her bouncy ponytail, faded blue jeans and navy hooded sweatshirt made her look like a college student rather than the thirtysomething professional he'd met yesterday. They also made her look way too appealing.

He quickly squelched that thought. "No, I've got to get this done before noon."

Ross shrugged. "Okay. Suit yourself." He turned and headed out the door.

Cam downed the last of his coffee, crushed his empty cup and threw it in the trash can. What was wrong with him? It would only take a few minutes to finish the framing project. There was plenty of time to help Rachel unload her truck. So, she was attractive. That didn't mean he had to stretch the truth to his friend and hide out in his shop like some kind of hermit.

Ross called out a greeting to Rachel, and the words floated back to Cam through the open window. He watched Ross jog out to meet her and take the box from her arms. She thanked him and flashed a killer smile.

Cam strained to hear their comments, but he couldn't catch the words.

Ross walked backward toward the building, toting the box and keeping an eye on Rachel as she returned to the truck.

Cam's frown deepened. What was up with that? Was Ross afraid she'd trip or something? Then it hit him—he was probably just enjoying the view.

Cam groaned and forced his gaze back to his work. Grabbing the power screwdriver from the shelf, he lined up the D-hook and positioned the screw. His hands stilled as he heard them enter the building.

Ross made a joke about needing backup lights to avoid a collision. Rachel laughed, sending a clear message she was enjoying Ross's help. Neither of them looked Cam's way when they passed his open door.

He clenched his jaw and drove the screw into the frame. It didn't matter. She had the help she needed.

Ross would take care of her. That's what he wanted, right?

Cam continued working, but he kept an eye on Rachel and Ross as they made three more trips to the truck. The fourth time outside, they scooted a large metal desk toward the tailgate. When they reached the edge, Ross hopped down to survey the situation and give Rachel directions.

Cam stared out the window. The old desk must weigh a ton. What was Ross thinking? Did he expect Rachel to help him haul that thing inside?

He set aside the screwdriver, then dashed out the door. His footsteps pounded down the hall, while his thoughts bounced back and forth like a crazy tennis ball.

He did not want to get involved with Rachel Clark.

Moving furniture into her office was not *getting involved*. He was simply helping out, doing the right thing. What could be wrong with doing what was right?

A lot!

Rachel strained forward, shoving the desk toward the tailgate. Oh brother, she was going to feel this tomorrow. She should've listened to her friend, Suzanne, and left it at the church. That would've been the smart thing to do.

But, once again, she didn't do the smart thing.

Ross jumped down from the truck, then looked up at her. "I think we can angle it down and slide it off the back." He motioned with his hands, demonstrating the process.

Rachel suppressed a smile. Ross Peterson was about as sweet as they come, but he obviously didn't have much experience moving furniture. If she tipped this desk over the edge and he tried to catch it, he would end up like a squished beetle on the sidewalk.

She straightened and wiped her sweaty hands on her pants' legs. "I don't know. It's pretty heavy. Maybe I should—"

"Wait!" Cam jogged down the sidewalk toward them. He sent Ross a scathing glance. "What are you trying to do, kill her?"

Rachel blinked. He was worried about her? Ross was the one about to be flattened by this overweight hunk of steel.

"We were just going to ease it out and slide it to the ground," Ross said.

Cam shook his head. "Not a good idea. Come on down, Rachel." He held out his hand to her.

She hesitated a split second, then took it and jumped down, hoping for a graceful landing. She wobbled slightly. His warm, sturdy grip tightened. Their gazes locked, and awareness zinged along her nerves.

He dropped her hand and spun away. "Come on, Ross."

The lanky photographer jumped forward and grabbed one side, while Cam gripped the other. They tugged the desk out over the edge, then tilted it and slowly lowered it to the ground. Cam moved to the opposite end, and the two men hoisted it in the air.

"Want me to take a corner?" Rachel asked.

"No! Get the door," Cam puffed as he and Ross hustled past.

"Okay." She ran up the steps and opened the door just in time for them to pass through. Sweat glistened on both men's foreheads, and they panted in time with their steps. Once inside, they slowed and Ross adjusted his grip on the desk.

"You got it?" Cam barked, deep lines creasing his forehead.

"Yea, but this'll probably give me a hernia."

Rachel blew out a deep breath. Oh, why hadn't she ditched that desk and bought one of those inexpensive, snap-together models that come in a box? Or she could've checked the classifieds and found a used one…anything would be lighter than this monster.

The men rounded the corner and headed down the hall toward her new office. Ross groaned, his end almost dragging on the floor.

"Don't drop it!" Cam grunted and raised his side higher.

Ross glared at Cam and kept shuffling along.

Rachel scurried ahead and opened the door. Boxes littered the floor. She hustled inside and pushed them aside to make a clear path.

"Where do you want this?" Cam looked over his shoulder as he backed through the doorway.

"Over here by the filing cabinet." She pointed to the corner, not wanting to add one extra step to their journey.

Cam led the way to the far side of the room and looked back at her with a lift of his brow.

The desk was a bit too close to the wall, but she wasn't about to redirect them now. "That's fine."

Ross dropped his end to the floor with a bang, startling them all. Cam swayed under the load. Rachel rushed forward to help. Cam lurched, and the desk landed on his toe. His eye's widened, and his mouth formed a perfect O, but no sound came out.

Rachel gasped and grabbed the desk, lifting the end a few inches off the ground. Cam jerked his foot out and hobbled to the window, silently clenching his fists.

Rachel shuddered and closed her eyes. Now Cam had another reason to hate her.

Rachel pushed the filing cabinet closer to the corner, then stood back to take a look. Perfect. She brushed off her hands and scanned her new office with a satisfied smile.

It had only taken about two hours to move in, much less time than she'd expected. Ross and Cam had certainly gone out of their way to help. After they left, she'd managed to shove her desk over a few more inches so it wouldn't be in the way when she opened her filing cabinet. Then she'd unpacked her files and books and set up her desk.

She bit her lip and leaned back against her desk. Too bad the desk had landed on Cam's toes. She'd apologized profusely—after she'd given him a few seconds to cool off. He'd insisted he was fine. But the way he limped out to get the last few boxes made it clear his foot hurt more than he'd let on. When they finished carrying in the boxes, he silently retreated to his shop, leaving her wondering if he'd ever speak to her again.

There must be some way she could make up for those crushed toes.

The faint scent of cinnamon floated through the air toward her. She glanced at the rectangular pan sitting by the window. The afternoon sunlight shone on the foil probably warming the cinnamon rolls to the perfect temperature. She'd brought them along in case some of her drama students stopped by to see the new location.

Maybe she'd pay Cam a little visit and bring him a peace offering. After all, weren't homemade cinnamon rolls a sure way into the good graces of any man?

She peeked in the mirror she'd hung on the wall moments before and shook her head. Her ponytail had come loose, and several strands of hair hung around her face.

That would never do. She pulled off the elastic band and grabbed a brush from her purse. After a quick brushing, she gathered her hair up in one hand and surveyed her reflection. She sucked in her cheeks and made a silly fish face, then let her hair go and brushed it out again. That was better.

She huffed and rolled her eyes. Why was she so concerned about how she looked? She was simply going to deliver the cinnamon rolls and try to bridge the gap between her and Cam before it grew any wider.

Right. Who was she trying to fool? Cam was an attractive man, in a mysterious, moody kind of way. She smiled, remembering how he looked hefting the heavy desk out of the truck. He was obviously strong and fit, and he'd come running when she needed help today.

But she was definitely not going to let herself get carried away with any romantic daydreams about him. She had no idea where he stood spiritually. And that was much more important to her than outward appearance or superficial kindness. Investing in a relationship that was destined to go nowhere was a bad idea. She'd made that mistake before, and suffered for it.

She tossed the hairbrush back in her purse. This whole line of thinking was silly. Even if Cam turned out to be a spiritual giant, he obviously didn't like her or the idea of having her kids in the building. As far as she could tell, they had nothing in common. And with his tight-lipped attitude, getting to know him any better seemed like a remote possibility.

Even a pan of homemade cinnamon rolls wasn't going to change that.

Chapter Five

"What do you think of this one?" Ross held up a 16 by 20 black-and-white photo of an old man and his bulldog watching an Alaska-bound ferry depart from the dock.

"I like it." Cam settled on the tall stool behind his workbench. "Looks like he wishes he was leaving on that ferry instead of being left behind."

Ross nodded. "I was thinking of a pearl-gray mat, about three inches, with a simple black frame."

"Sounds good." Cam pulled three corner-shaped frame samples from the wall behind him. Footsteps approached, and he glanced toward the door.

Rachel stepped into view carrying a foil-covered pan. She'd taken down her ponytail, and her dark hair brushed her shoulders. Her brown eyes glowed as she sent him a hesitant smile.

Cam swallowed and shifted his gaze away.

"Hi. I thought you guys might like a snack."

"Sure." Ross motioned her into the shop. "What've you got there?"

"Cinnamon rolls." She crossed the room and set the pan on the workbench.

Cam frowned. Sticky icing was the last thing he wanted in his workspace.

"Sounds great." Ross hovered nearby as she pulled off the foil. "Wow, are those homemade?"

She nodded, a slight blush filling her cheeks. "Well, sort of. I made the dough in a bread machine."

Ross rubbed his hands together. "Hey, that's home-made in my book."

Cam leaned forward slightly and pulled in a deep breath. They smelled great and looked even better.

"I thought we might need these." Rachel pulled a wad of white paper napkins from her jeans pocket and laid them on the workbench. "You want to try one?"

Cam's empty stomach gurgled. "Sure. Thanks."

Gooey icing dripped down the side as she passed him a large fluffy roll. He took a bite, and cinnamon sweetness burst on his tongue. Closing his eyes, he let the buttery roll melt in his mouth. Man, oh man, this was amazing.

Ross bit into his roll and moaned. "Oh. My. Good-ness! You should go into business. No, wait. Don't let anyone taste these. Save them all for me."

She laughed. "So you like them?"

Ross grinned and nodded.

"Mmm-hmm," Cam mumbled, his neck warming as he took another bite.

A slow smile tucked in the corners of her mouth. She cut a roll in half and joined them. Ross asked her when the drama classes would start. She gave him the rundown, while Cam licked his fingers and took the second half of her cinnamon roll from the pan.

"Once summer classes and rehearsals begin it would save me a lot of driving time if I could find a place of my own down here."

"Where are you staying now?" Ross asked.

"Up in North Bellingham with a friend." She wiped her mouth with a napkin. "Do you guys know anyone who has an apartment for rent in this area?"

Panic flashed along Cam's nerves, and he shot a warning glance at Ross, but his friend was focused on Rachel.

"We sure do." Ross patted Cam on the shoulder. "Cam's been renovating the second floor of his house into a separate apartment." He glanced at Cam. "You're almost done, aren't you?"

Cam shook his head and tried to choke down his last bite of cinnamon roll. "No. No, I'm still working on the bathroom and kitchen." Renting the apartment to Rachel would be a bad idea.

Ross narrowed his eyes. "I thought you said all

you have left is caulking around the tub and putting up some molding in the kitchen."

"Yeah…but…I'm sure Rachel wouldn't be interested." Not unless she saw it, and that wasn't happening.

"I might be. What's it like?"

Cam walked over to the sink and rinsed his hands. "Well…it's old and has some odd-shaped rooms." His house was great. But he wasn't about to tell her that.

"Cam's just being modest," Ross added without missing a beat. "He's done an amazing job. Refinished the hardwood floors and put in a totally new kitchen."

Rachel's eyes lit up. "Wow, I'm impressed."

Ross nodded. "It has two bedrooms, a nice-sized living room and new, energy-saving windows. And just think, your landlord would be right downstairs if you need anything."

Cam stifled a moan and sunk down on the stool behind his workbench. He was going to kill Ross.

Rachel's eyes glowed. "It sounds wonderful."

Great! How was he going to get out of this one? He shifted his gaze to Ross, wishing he could stuff the wad of napkins in his friend's mouth.

Ross finally looked his way. Understanding dawned in his eyes, and his smile deflated.

"Is it far from here?" Rachel asked.

Ross quietly wiped his hands on a napkin.

Cam shifted on the stool. "About five minutes."

"Oh, that would be perfect. I'd love to see it." She hesitated, looking back and forth between them. "I mean, if you're open to showing it to me."

He clenched his jaw. What choice did he have? "Sure."

"How about tomorrow?"

He shook his head. Maybe he could delay her, and she'd find something else. "I'm going down to Seattle for the day." He hadn't seen his sister, Shannon, and her family for a couple months. Maybe he'd pay them a visit.

"What about Sunday?"

He rubbed his chin, trying to think of another excuse, but none came to mind. "I suppose that would be okay. How about 9:00 a.m.?" Maybe she liked to sleep in on the weekend and would turn him down.

"I'll be at church in the morning, but I could come around one."

His face flamed. Of course he should have known she'd be in church. "One is fine," he muttered.

"Great. I can't wait to see it. Could you write down the address for me?"

He walked over to his desk and jotted it down, then handed her the paper.

"Thanks." As she studied the address, Cam looked past her shoulder and glared at Ross. How many years would he get for murdering his best friend?

* * *

Rachel followed the sidewalk around the side of the large Craftsman-style house, admiring the soft-gray and frosty-cranberry paint job. Very nice.

The house boasted a large central gable, low-pitched roof and a huge front porch upheld by two square pillars. It was charming in a sturdy, masculine kind of way. If the interior was half as nice as what she saw outside, she'd take it—if Cam would rent to her and if she could afford it. Those were some very big ifs.

When Ross mentioned the apartment to her on Friday, Cam had about gagged on his cinnamon roll. He'd tried to hide his reaction, but she'd seen right through him.

Why did he dislike her so much? Was it just that she was bringing kids into the Arts Center? Did he see that as some kind of threat? Or was there something else about her that bothered him?

Well, it didn't matter how he felt about her and her kids. She needed this apartment. And after pouring over the classifieds for the last few days and talking to a real estate agent, she discovered there weren't too many other options in this area, especially in her price range.

With a silent prayer on her lips, she climbed the stairs to the small side porch and knocked on the door. Her stomach did a jumpy little dance while she waited.

The door opened and Cam greeted her with a smile that looked forced. He wore a paint-spattered navy T-shirt and faded jeans with a hole in one knee. A few white paint speckles dotted his glasses.

"Come in." He motioned toward the stairs, his stiff posture shouting his discomfort. "This is a private entrance to the apartment."

"That's convenient." She mounted the stairs, and the top landing came into view. A pendant-shaped light fixture made of stained glass spread a warm glow over the gleaming hardwood floor, creamy walls and beamed ceiling. "Wow, this is lovely."

He frowned slightly and rubbed his hands on his jeans. "Well, like I said, I'm not totally finished."

"What you've done so far looks great. Can I see the rest?"

He nodded and led her into the kitchen. "I gutted this room." He motioned toward the new oak cabinets and stainless-steel appliances.

"It's beautiful." Rachel's heart lifted as she walked over to a large bay window and looked outside. She imagined herself sitting at her breakfast table, enjoying the view of the beautiful backyard with its brick patio and neat vegetable garden. She turned back to Cam. "Did you do all of this work yourself?"

"Most of it. But I used professionals for the electric and plumbing."

She nodded and ran her hand over the granite counter, noticing how it coordinated with the tile backsplash and floor. "I've never seen tile like this."

"It's from Italy."

She cocked her head. "You know, most people wouldn't invest so much in a place they were going to rent to someone else."

He shrugged. "Quality materials will last. And I intend to find a renter who will take care of the apartment as if it was their own." He sent her a serious look, then continued the tour through the rest of the apartment. She asked him several questions and praised his craftsmanship and attention to detail in each room. He seemed to relax and soften a bit as he showed her around.

When they returned to the landing, she stopped and looked up. "I love that light fixture. It adds a nice touch. It would look great with an oriental rug in those same colors." She imagined her small chest with the potted fern against one wall and her tall bookshelf against the other.

She pulled in a deep breath, wishing she didn't have to ask the next question. "So...how much is the rent?"

He folded his arms across his broad chest and named the price.

She swallowed and released a soft sigh. "I guess I should've asked that before I came."

He frowned and rubbed his chin. "You think it's too much?"

"No, it's definitely worth it. It's just too much for me."

He slipped his hands in his pockets and lifted his gaze to meet hers. "Are you sure?"

Surprise rippled through her. He almost sounded like he wanted to rent the apartment to her. She nodded slowly, wishing she could give him another answer. "By the time I paid rent and utilities, I'd be eating oatmeal three times a day and have to walk to work."

"Oh…the utilities are included in the rent."

"Really?" Her hopes rebounded.

"Yes. I'll cover the electric, gas and water, and I have wireless Internet that works all over the house."

"That would be great." She bit her lip and did some quick calculations. "I'm sure I could handle the payments then."

A nervous smile broke over his face. "So…you want to rent it?"

"Yes. Definitely. It's much nicer than anything else I've seen."

He nodded, growing serious again. "Okay, maybe you could give me a couple references and contact info for your last landlord."

"Sure. I brought that information with me."

He shifted his weight from one foot to the other. "I guess we could go downstairs and take care of that now."

"Okay." She followed him down the steps, slowing to admire a tall window with a section of stained glass at the top. Sunlight streamed through the red, blue and amber design, creating a pattern on the opposite wall. "That's lovely."

He glanced over his shoulder at the window. "It's original to the house. Not airtight like the new windows, but I couldn't tear it out."

"I'm glad you didn't." Their gazes connected and held, and awareness tingled through her. She looked away, breaking the connection. Maybe this wasn't such a good idea after all. She'd have to be very careful to guard her heart and not fall for her handsome landlord.

Cam hustled up his porch steps and pushed open the front door for Rachel. His golden retriever ran forward to greet them with a sharp bark and a series of vigorous wiggles and tail wagging that about knocked Rachel over. She stepped behind Cam.

"Whoa! Down, girl." He grabbed the dog's collar. "Sorry. She won't hurt you. She's just trying to make friends."

The hint of panic in Rachel's eyes faded, and she sent him a tentative smile. "What's her name?"

"Sasha." He looked the dog in the eye. "Settle down and be nice." He glanced up at Rachel. "Hold out your hand, and let her sniff it."

Rachel bit her lip and slowly extended her hand,

looking as though she believed Sasha might eat her for lunch.

He suppressed a smile. "I take it you're not used to dogs?"

"Not really, but she seems nice." Sasha licked Rachel's palm, then nuzzled closer and gazed up at her with soulful eyes. "Oh, you're a pretty girl, aren't you?" Rachel's voice took on that soft quality people use when they talk to babies and small animals. She laughed, and gently ran her hand over the dog's back.

Sasha's tongue hung out the side of her mouth in a slobbery dog smile while her long tail beat time on the carpet.

"She likes you." He grinned, watching them get acquainted. They made quite a nice picture—Rachel in her slim navy and white dress topped with a navy cardigan. It followed her feminine curves and skimmed the top of her knees, revealing tan shapely legs below.

What was not to like? He swallowed and quickly raised his gaze to her face.

"She's so soft." Rachel tipped her head and looked up at him with glowing eyes and a sweet smile.

The room suddenly felt too warm. He cleared his throat and stepped back. "Let me…a…grab that rental application." He turned away and headed toward the desk in the dining room.

What was he doing? Before she arrived, he'd

made up his mind to discourage her from renting the apartment. But that was before she praised his remodeling work in every room and knocked down all his defenses. By the time he finished showing her around, his resistance had vanished, and he'd adjusted the rent to include the utilities.

That was crazy! He had to stop being such a pushover. It was bad enough that he was going to see her every day at work. Now she was going to be his upstairs neighbor?

Maybe he'd find something negative in her references or credit check. But he doubted that. She had a good job. He couldn't imagine her having credit issues. She practically glowed with integrity. If everything came back as he expected, he'd have to rent the apartment to her. Gritting his teeth, he fished through the drawer for a decent pen.

Maybe he was looking at this wrong. Renting to Rachel would be better than having a couple upstairs, or worse yet, a family with young kids. He huffed out an irritated breath and walked back into the living room with the forms and pen in hand.

Rachel stood by the fireplace looking at a framed photo on the mantel of him with his wife and son.

His stomach clenched, and he wished he'd followed his earlier inclination to put it away. Explaining their absence was the last thing he wanted to do.

She turned, questions in her eyes. "You used to have a beard."

He nodded, but there was more on her mind than that. His gaze flicked from the photo to Rachel's expectant face. He might as well tell her the truth and get it out of the way. Not the whole truth, of course—just enough to stop her questions. "That's my wife, Marie, and our son, Tyler."

She lifted her brows. "I didn't realize you were married."

He clenched his jaw and tried to swallow. "They... died four years ago in a car accident. We were hit by a drunk driver."

Compassion replaced the question in her eyes. "Oh...I'm sorry. I didn't mean to—"

He lifted his hand. "No. It's okay." He didn't want her sympathy. He didn't deserve it.

She dropped her gaze and rubbed her arms, obviously uncomfortable with the turn in their conversation.

He handed her the application forms and motioned to the couch. "You can sit down and fill them out now if you like."

"Okay. Thanks." She took a seat, then pulled a small notebook from her purse and began copying reference information onto the first sheet.

He rubbed Sasha's head. "I hope you don't mind if I run a credit check."

She glanced up at him, her brown eyes still reflecting empathy. "No. That's fine. There shouldn't be any problems."

There was a twenty-dollar fee for that, but for some reason he decided not to charge her.

A few minutes later she stood and handed him the completed forms. "Here you go." She slipped the notebook back in her purse. "I do have one more question. Do you need a security deposit?"

"Yes, it's one and a half month's rent." His friend who was a realtor had coached him on all this.

Her shoulders sagged slightly as she set the pen on the table.

He couldn't stand the look of disappointment in her eyes. "If that's a problem, we could do half the first month and half the second."

Her face brightened. "Thanks. That would really help. I've been making extra payments on my grad school loans, and things are a little tight right now."

"I'll run the credit check, contact your references and get back to you in a few days."

"Okay." She held out her hand to him. "Thanks. I love the apartment."

When he grasped her hand, a warm, melting sensation traveled up his arm. As he tightened his grip and looked into her eyes, he made his decision. Even if her reference and credit check weren't perfect, he'd found his tenant.

Chapter Six

"It's just around the corner, number seventy-two." Rachel checked the house numbers, certain she'd recognize Cam's place as soon as it came into view.

"Is that it?" Josh Crocker, her friend Suzanne's husband, slowed his black truck and nodded toward the house.

"Yes." Rachel surveyed the big front porch and neat yard. It looked even more inviting than she remembered from her visit last Sunday. Leaves had unfurled on the big maple tree out front, and purple iris bloomed in the flowerbed along the driveway.

Cam hustled down the porch steps and tossed a red Frisbee to Sasha. She dashed across the yard and leaped in the air to snag it, then raced back to Cam.

Josh pulled the truck into the driveway, and Rachel's stomach fluttered. Was she excited about finally having her own place, or did it have more to do with seeing her handsome landlord again? A shiver raced up her back, and she scolded herself. Cam hadn't given the slightest hint he was interested in being anything more than her co-op partner and landlord. And even those connections seemed an uncomfortable stretch for him.

Climbing out of the truck, she recalled how she'd spent the first half of the week anxiously waiting to hear if he would rent the apartment to her. They'd only crossed paths twice at the Arts Center, but he hadn't said anything, so she didn't bring it up. She didn't want to rush him or make him feel awkward about the situation.

He'd finally called Thursday afternoon to say her references and credit were fine, and she could move in that weekend. She'd done a happy dance all around the kitchen and celebrated by making a special lasagna dinner for Suzanne and Josh. Then Suzanne sat with her while she packed her suitcase with the few items she kept at their house. All her furniture and boxes had been in storage since she moved from Seattle to Fairhaven five months earlier.

Rachel smiled thinking of the treasures in the back of Josh's truck. It would feel like Christmas opening all her boxes today. Not that her belongings would be worth much to anyone else, but to her, they symbolized her independence and a fresh start in Fairhaven.

Josh grabbed his baseball hat off the dashboard. "You ready to go?"

"Yes!" She hopped out of the truck and crossed the yard to greet Cam. Josh ambled over and joined them. Rachel introduced the men.

Josh smiled and held out his hand to Cam. "Good to meet you."

Cam nodded and looked Josh over with a glint of disapproval in his eyes. He finally shook Josh's hand.

What was Cam's problem? How could he dislike Josh? He'd just met the man.

A horn honked. Rachel turned as a silver Mustang pulled in the driveway and parked behind Josh's truck. Ryan Hoffman, Steve Conover and Haley Mitchell, three of Rachel's teenage drama students, piled out of the car.

"The movers have arrived," Ryan announced. Seventeen, tall and athletic, Ryan was a natural leader among the group.

"Hey, Ms. Clark." Haley waved and tossed her long brown hair over her shoulder. Haley's beautiful voice and sweet spirit often won her leading roles in the N.C.Y.T. musicals, and she wasn't afraid to get her hands dirty when it came time to paint sets or clean up after a production.

Steve was a natural comic. He grinned and lifted his sunglasses to the top of his head, then nodded toward the house. "Nice place. You're really moving up in the world, Ms. Clark."

"Hey, watch it." Josh gave Steve a playful punch in the arm. "My place is not that bad."

Cam's scowl deepened, and he glared at Josh, clearly perturbed about something.

Rachel stepped in front of Cam. "Great to see you guys. Thanks for coming." Her students were well acquainted with Josh, so she introduced them to Cam. His expression softened, and he seemed to let go of whatever was bothering him.

As they walked back toward the truck to collect the first load of boxes, Josh leaned her way. "What's up with your landlord? Looks like he swallowed a jar of sour pickles."

"Sorry. I have no idea what set him off." She huffed and shook her head. Moodiness was one thing, but rudeness was another.

Josh chuckled. "Don't worry about it. I probably remind him of some guy who beat him up in sixth grade."

"Maybe that's it." She sent him a teasing grin. "But don't worry, I still love you."

"Good thing." He slipped his arm around her shoulder and gave her a playful squeeze.

She laughed and poked him in the side.

He jumped back. "Hey! You better be nice if you want me to cart all this stuff upstairs."

She held up her hands. "Okay, okay. I'll be good. I promise."

Cam scowled at them, then called Sasha and put her inside.

Three hours later, Cam stopped at the bottom of Rachel's stairs and rubbed his lower back. He thought he was in pretty good shape, but toting all of Rachel's furniture up those stairs had been a huge job, even with five other people helping. Hopefully, they were almost finished. Steve and Ryan trotted past with a couple more big boxes.

"Are there any more out there?"

Ryan slowed on the first landing. "Yeah. One more. But Haley's got it."

Josh pounded down the step and met Cam on the small side porch. He leaned over the railing to gain a better view of the driveway. "Any more boxes out there?"

"No. This is it," Haley called as she carried the last one up the sidewalk.

Josh slapped Cam on the shoulder. "Well, guess we're just about done."

Cam cringed. "Yeah."

Josh cocked his head, looking as though he wanted to ask Cam a question, but then turned and jogged back upstairs.

Irritation crawled along Cam's hot, sweaty arms. What did Rachel see in that guy? Sure, he was friendly and was built like a weight lifter. But if he didn't have character and respect for Rachel, what good were those qualities? Cam growled under his breath and followed Josh through the door.

How could Rachel spout all that stuff about being a good example to her students and then live with her boyfriend? Talk about a double standard. It totally burst his bubble. Maybe he was old-fashioned, but he believed you should wait until you were married to live together.

Cam slowly climbed the stairs, trying to put together his first impression of Rachel with what he'd learned today. But they didn't jive. He joined everyone in the kitchen.

"You sure you don't want us to stick around and help you unpack boxes?" Josh leaned against the counter watching Rachel place glasses in the cabinet.

"No. I'll be fine. You guys have done more than enough. Besides, I'll feel more organized if I put it away myself." She reached for Josh and gave him a hug. Her petite size next to her hulking boyfriend sent another wave of frustration through Cam. Guys were supposed to love, serve and lead. He ought to protect her, not take advantage of her.

"Thanks for everything. I could never have done this without you." Rachel gave Josh a final squeeze.

"You're welcome." He stepped back. "You know, it's just not going to be the same without you."

Ryan and Haley exchanged a smile as they watched them. Cam rolled his eyes, barely able to hold back a gagging noise in his throat.

Rachel thanked her students and promised to invite them over as soon as she had the apartment organized. They called out their goodbyes and followed Josh down the stairs. Cam watched them go with a sad shake of his head. Didn't Rachel realize how impressionable teens were? How could she expect them to say no to peer pressure when she practically announced to the world she wasn't waiting for marriage.

Cam spotted Josh's red baseball cap on top of a box sitting by the bedroom doorway. He snatched it up, debating if he should run after the guy. He decided against it and sauntered into the kitchen instead. Rachel continued her unpacking, lifting a stack of dishes from a box.

He held out the red baseball cap between his thumb and forefinger like it was last week's garbage. "Your boyfriend left his hat."

"My what?" Rachel turned and looked at him with a baffled expression.

"Your boyfriend, Josh. This is his hat." He couldn't keep the disgust from his voice.

A slow smile broke over her face. "Josh isn't my boyfriend. He's married to Suzanne, my best friend.

She's the former director of N.C.Y.T. I've been staying with them for the last five months."

"He's married to your best friend?"

"Yes. Suzanne would've come today, but she's six months pregnant and needs to stay off her feet. Doctor's orders."

Heat flooded his neck and face. "So you guys are just friends." He blew out a deep breath and silently berated himself.

"Yes." She tossed a wad of packing paper in an empty box. "Suzanne and I were roommates in college. That's where she and Josh met. They got married right after graduation. We go to the same church now. We're really close, like family."

"Oh man. I treated that guy like dirt." He blew out a deep breath. "I thought you two were…you know… living together."

Rachel gasped and almost dropped a stack of plates. "No! I mean we lived in the same house, but we never—"

"I get it." He tossed the hat on the table and shook his head. "Josh probably thinks I'm a jerk."

She waved away his words, her eyes twinkling. She obviously wasn't too upset about his mistake. "I wouldn't worry about Josh. He's easygoing. I'll explain next time I see him."

"Thanks." He glanced around the kitchen, wondering if there was some way to put this embarrassing blunder out of her mind. "Are you hungry?"

"Starving."

"Do you like pizza?"

"My favorite."

"Okay. I'll be back in a few minutes." He headed down the steps and out the door. Stepping onto the side porch, he stopped and blew out a deep breath. His steps felt lighter, and his tiredness seemed to have disappeared. Maybe his bubble hadn't burst after all.

Rachel cut open the FedEx box and lifted out the top script for the new summer musical. A smile flooded her face as she scanned the cover. She loved the story of *Anne of Green Gables*. Something about the determined young heroine overcoming all odds spoke to her heart. She flipped the pages, reading snatches of dialog and stage direction. It was the perfect show for her group since most of the parts were for characters about the same age as her students.

The music and choreography would be challenging, but she had several talented kids who could pull it off with coaching from Jack Herman, the music director, and Chandra Wetzel, their choreographer.

"Morning, Rachel. How's it going?" Lilly Wong peeked in Rachel's office doorway.

"Great. Come in. We just got the new scripts for our summer musical."

Lilly glanced at the title and smiled. "Oh, I loved that movie."

"Me too."

"I did some baking last night. Thought I'd spread the calories around." Lilly handed her a small plate of brownies covered with plastic wrap.

"Thanks. Brownies are my favorite." She grinned. "Actually, anything chocolate is high on my list."

"Where have you been the last few days?" Lilly asked.

"I've been moving into my new apartment." Rachel set the tempting treats on her desk, determined to wait awhile before she had one. "And we're still holding after-school drama classes at Grace Community Church on Tuesdays and Thursdays."

"When do the classes start down here?" Lilly took a seat on the chair next to Rachel's desk.

"In a couple weeks, as soon as school's out." Rachel pushed the FedEx box aside and sat on the corner of her desk. "The kids are going to love it here. Having our own stage where we can build our sets while we rehearse is going to make it so much easier."

"I hope you're right about the parents shopping in our galleries."

Rachel smiled and nodded. "I'm sure you'll see an increase in business as soon as summer camp and rehearsals start."

"I wish I had your confidence." Lilly's smile faded. "It's been rough the last few months. If business doesn't improve soon, I don't think we're going to make it."

Rachel stared at Lilly. Was she talking about her own gallery or the whole Arts Center? "Really? Are things that bad?"

"I've used up most of my savings. If I don't make some profit this summer, I'll have to close my doors. And I'm afraid we're all in the same boat."

How could that be? When Rachel signed the lease she expected to be here for at least the next six months and hopefully longer. Cam had given her the impression the co-op's finances were in good shape with the added income from N.C.Y.T. Why hadn't he told her things were so tenuous? Irritation zinged along her nerves. She'd have to talk to him about it later.

Footsteps approached in the hallway. "Oh, there you are." Melanie Howard sauntered into Rachel's office wearing slim-cut designer jeans, an aqua sweater and a hand-painted silk scarf that reminded Rachel of one of Lilly's watercolors. Giving Rachel a brief nod, Melanie turned to Lilly. "Have you seen Cam? I was hoping to give him an update on the plant donations I've lined up." Her gaze flicked to Rachel. "I've just about got the list covered."

Rachel pulled in a sharp breath. Rats! She'd made several calls last week, but she hadn't connected with any garden centers willing to make the donations.

Well, Melanie might have beaten her to the punch

on the landscaping project, but she had some information Melanie didn't.

"Cam should be back around ten." Rachel glanced at her watch, trying not to look too smug. "He had a dentist appointment this morning."

Melanie lifted her brows. "Oh, really?"

Rachel nodded. "He broke a tooth last night. Good thing the dentist could see him first thing this morning. It was pretty painful."

Melanie's eyes widened. "Last night?"

"Yes." Rachel suppressed a smile. Obviously Melanie liked Cam. Did he return her interest? Rachel hadn't noticed any nonverbal connection between them, but she had only observed them in the same room two or three times.

"So, you two were together last night?" Lilly asked with a delighted grin. "Tell us more."

Rachel hesitated. There wasn't really much more to tell, but seeing the shocked expression on Melanie's face, she couldn't resist carrying this just a little further.

"Cam helped me move into my new apartment." She gave a coy shrug of her shoulders. "We were both hungry after that, so he ordered pizza and Cokes. Unfortunately, he chewed on an ice cube and broke his tooth." She sighed and shook her head. "My dentist always told me never chew on ice. I should've warned him."

Lilly tilted her head. "Wow. He helped you move, and then ordered pizza?"

"Yes. Wasn't that thoughtful?" Rachel couldn't hide her smile any longer.

A nerve in Melanie's jaw twitched. "Yes. Very." Her tone was as cold and jagged as a chunk of ice.

Rachel's stomach tightened. She wasn't really being dishonest, just letting them come to their own conclusions. Still, she shouldn't give them the wrong impression about her and Cam. What if it got back to him? How would she explain?

Just then, Cam walked in the door.

Her stomach dropped as if she'd just ridden a fast elevator from the top floor to the basement in five seconds flat.

Chapter Seven

Cam glanced around the room at the three women. Rachel's eyes widened, and the color drained from her face. Lilly tucked her hand in her skirt pockets and bit her lip as she frowned at the floor. Melanie crossed her arms and glared at him like he'd stomped on her cat's tail.

He had definitely walked into the middle of something.

"So, how's the tooth?" Melanie asked.

He shot a glance at Rachel, and then reached up and rubbed his frozen jaw. So they'd been talking about him. "It's okay. Still feels pretty numb, but I'll live."

Rachel cringed slightly, as though the broken tooth was her fault. It wasn't, but he appreciated her sympathy.

He reached into his pants pocket and fingered the copy of the apartment key. He'd stopped in to give it to Rachel. But glancing at Lilly and Melanie, he decided now might not be the right time.

Melanie's sour expression made him wonder if she already knew Rachel was now his upstairs neighbor.

"Well, we better get back to work." Lilly took Melanie's arm and tugged her toward the door.

Melanie scowled at Lilly, but gave in and followed along. "I'll stop in and see you later, Cam. I need to talk to you about the plant donations for the landscaping project."

"I'm headed home. How about tomorrow?"

"All right. I'll stop by tomorrow morning." She wiggled her fingers at him. "Bye."

Cam waited until they left, then took the key from his pocket and held it out to Rachel. "I got this copy made for you on my way back from the dentist."

"Thanks. But…why don't you keep the new one, and I'll hold on to the one you gave me last night."

"Okay." He dropped the shiny new key into his pocket. "So…is everything okay with Melanie and Lilly?"

Her eyes widened. "Yes. Sure. Everything's fine. No problem at all." She looked around, snatched the plate of brownies, and held it out to him. "Would you like a brownie? Lilly made them."

"No thanks." He tapped his numb jaw. "Don't think I could taste anything right now."

"Oh. Yes. Of course. You should probably wait

awhile before you eat anything." She studied his face for a moment, concern filling her eyes again. "Sorry about your tooth."

"Hey, it's okay. I'm a tough guy." He chuckled, then rubbed his upper arm. "Except after a day of hauling boxes and furniture to the second floor. You should've warned me that you have a huge book collection."

She laughed, looking relieved, and it was the nicest sound he'd heard in a long time.

"Knock, knock," Melanie called.

Cam stifled a groan and looked up from his computer. "Hey, Melanie."

She sauntered into the shop and sent him a slow, suggestive smile. Her clothes looked fine, but he couldn't help noticing the large clumps of navy, green and pink beads dangling from her ears. They hung so low they almost touched her shoulders. Must be one of her new designs.

How could she stand having something that heavy hanging from her earlobes? Didn't they get in the way when she turned her head? And if the earrings weren't enough, she wore a matching necklace and bracelet. The whole heavy jewelry thing made him glad he was a man, and he didn't have to deal with that kind of nonsense.

"Wait until you hear my news." She laid a file folder on his desk and pulled up a chair so she could sit next to him, her beads jangling the whole time. A cloud of musky perfume settled around them as she scooted her chair closer.

Cam sat back and tried not to breathe too deeply.

She nodded toward the file. "Go ahead. Open it."

He did and found a list of donors and plants for the landscaping project. "Looks good." He ran his finger down the page. "What about the larkspur and columbine? Do you think you'll be able to get those?"

A slight pout replaced her smile. "I thought you'd be happy to see how much I've done." When that had no effect on him, her smile resurfaced. "I'll make a few more calls. I'm sure I can get the rest. Paxton's Garden Center is the main donor. They said they'd deliver and give us some free mulch. Isn't that great?" She gazed at him expectantly. "When do you want it delivered?"

At this close range he could see she wore contacts and way too much makeup. He rolled his chair back and got up. "Let me talk to Ross and the others about a date for a work party, then we can schedule the delivery."

His thoughts shifted to Rachel, and he frowned slightly. Hadn't she promised to work on plant donations? Why hadn't she followed through? Maybe she was all talk and no action. He shouldn't be surprised.

She probably wasn't as committed as everyone else. Still, he had expected more from her.

A squeal of laughter from the hallway pierced his thoughts, followed by the sound of running feet and more laughter. Cam scowled. What was going on?

Two young boys dashed by—at least he thought it was two young boys. They ran so fast it was hard to tell.

Melanie spun toward the door. "What in the world?"

The boys darted by again, calling out as one chased the other in the opposite direction. Their squeaking tennis shoes, pounding footsteps and high-pitched voices echoed off the walls and tile floor, making the hair stand up on the back of Cam's neck.

Melanie clicked her tongue. "Where are their parents?"

"I don't know, but I intend to find out." Cam got up and strode out the door. Following the boys' voices, he rounded the corner and found them at the water fountain, one boy gleefully squirting the other. A fast-spreading puddle of water surrounded their feet.

"Hey!" Cam hustled toward them. "What do you think you're doing?"

The boys froze and looked at him through large blue eyes. Water dripped down their faces onto their T-shirts and shorts.

Cam squinted. One boy wore a blue shirt and the

other red, but their faces were identical. "I asked you boys a question."

The twins exchanged nervous glances. "We were just getting a drink," the boy on the left in the red shirt said.

"Right." Cam scoffed. "You were doing a whole lot more than that and you know it. Where are your parents?"

"They're at work." The boy on the right spoke this time, his chin quivering. "We're here with our sister."

"Where is she?"

Both boys pointed down the hall past Cam's shoulder. "She's talking to Ms. Clark," the boy in the blue shirt said.

Heat flashed into Cam's face, and he clenched his jaw. These must be two of Rachel's drama students. "Let's go." He grabbed the boys by their soggy shirt-sleeves and towed them back toward Rachel's office. "You and Ms. Clark have some explaining to do."

The boy on his left began to sniff. "We didn't mean to get the floor wet."

"We just wanted a drink," the other boy added in a whiny voice.

Cam opened Rachel's door and marched them into the room.

Rachel stood near her desk with the three teens who had helped her move into her apartment. She stopped mid-sentence and turned to him. "What's going on?"

He crossed his arms and narrowed his eyes at her. "That's what I'd like to know."

"Why are you guys all wet?" Haley asked.

"We just stopped to get a drink of water." The boy in the blue shirt held out his hands. "We didn't mean to get water on the floor."

Haley gasped. "Brian! I told you guys to go straight to the bathroom and come right back." She crossed the room and stood in front of her brothers.

Brian dropped his chin and refused to look at her.

Haley turned to the other twin. "Jeff? Tell me what happened."

"Brian started it. He squirted me."

Brian's head popped up. "Well, you squirted me back!"

"I did not!"

"Yes you did!"

"I'm soaked!"

"That's your fault!"

Haley held up her hand. "Guys! Stop!"

"The point is," Cam said with a definite edge to his voice. "These boys were running through the halls and having a water fight at the drinking fountain."

Rachel opened her mouth, no doubt intending to argue with him, but he was not about to listen to any excuses.

He pointed an accusing finger at her. "You promised your students wouldn't cause any problems." His voice grew more strident as he continued. "Summer camp hasn't even started, and they're already making trouble."

Fire flashed in Rachel's eyes. The twins quivered in their soggy tennis shoes. Ryan, Steve and Haley stared at him like he was some kind of evil villain.

"I'm sorry, Ms. Clark," Haley said. "I should've walked them to the bathroom." She laid her hand on her brothers' shoulders. "Come on. Lets go clean up the mess."

"We'll help." Ryan looked at Steve and nodded toward the door. His friend picked up the cue, and they followed Haley and the twins into the hall.

"You'll find a mop in the janitor's closet just past the drinking fountain," Cam called.

Rachel watched the kids hurry out the door. When she was certain they were out of earshot she spun around. "How could you treat those children like that?"

"*Those children* need to learn there are consequences for destructive behavior."

"I would hardly call getting a little water on the floor destructive behavior."

"Well it would've been a flood if I hadn't stopped them."

"Don't you think you are exaggerating just a little?"

"The issue is you promised to supervise your students, and you failed to keep that promise."

She sucked in a quick breath. "Those boys aren't my students. They're too young for our program."

"It's still your responsibility to keep an eye on them."

"We sent them to the bathroom. I had no idea they'd get distracted on the way."

"The water fight started after they ran screaming down the hall. I can't believe you didn't hear them."

"My door was shut!"

"Oh, well, that explains it." He huffed. "Maybe you should've kept it open so you could hear what's going on."

"Look, I never promised every child who enters the building would never speak above a whisper!"

He leaned toward her, his intensity matching hers. "And I never said I expected silence. I just asked you to keep your kids under control and not tear the building apart!"

She clenched her jaw. "All right. I get the point."

"Good. Because if this is going to work, you've got to do a better job overseeing your kids."

His words cut through her like a knife. "A better job?"

"Yes. Be in charge. Supervise what's going on. Take your promise seriously."

Her mouth dropped open. Of all the rude, pompous things to say! How could he make such sweeping judgments about her based on one small incident. A flaming rebuttal rose in her throat, but there was too much at risk to blurt it out now, no matter how unfair his words were. She grabbed her purse off the desk. "I…I can't talk about this right now."

Without looking back, she rushed out the door. But she couldn't run away from the memory of his brooding scowl.

The gray, wind-whipped waters of Bellingham Bay came into view as Rachel traveled west on Taylor Avenue. Dancing whitecaps ruffled the surface of the harbor, and threatening clouds rose in the west. The rain hadn't started yet, but a storm seemed only moments away.

Rachel scanned the sky, certain the weather was a perfect reflection of her life. A downpour of trouble was due to dump on her at any moment, and no umbrella was going to keep her from being soaked this time.

Why had she ever promised Cam she would keep her kids quiet and never disturb anyone? Who was she kidding? Keeping two rambunctious boys under control for ten minutes had proven impossible. What was she going to do when all fifty kids showed up for summer drama camp? Had she locked herself into an impossible situation that was doomed for failure? Would she end up losing her lease at the Arts Center before summer camp even began?

Straightening her shoulders, she pulled in a calming breath. Whatever it took, she had to find a way to make this work. There was no other option.

She rolled to a stop at the corner and tapped on the steering wheel as she waited to make a left turn. Perhaps things weren't really as bleak as they seemed. Not all of her co-op partners were so difficult to please…just a certain frame shop owner who needed to lighten up and learn how to take things in stride.

Kids made noise! Their energy, laughter and goofy antics were going to disrupt the peaceful ambience of the Arts Center. Their music and dancing might even shake the walls of that old building, but that wasn't necessarily a bad thing. He just needed to adjust his expectations.

She parked near the Taylor Avenue dock and climbed out of the car. Perhaps a stroll on the South Bay Trail would clear her head and give her a chance to pray through everything.

A wave of conviction washed over her, slowing her racing thoughts. It was past time she consulted the One who knew how to resolve this situation rather than plowing ahead under her own steam and running straight into more trouble.

A cool, salt-tinged wind blew the hair away from her face as she trudged toward the dock and path that ran north through Boulevard Park up the South Bay Trail from Fairhaven to Bellingham proper.

Gulls hung on the breeze circling the sailboats anchored in the harbor. One lone walker in purple capri pants and matching sweatshirt strode toward her, a hot pink sun visor shading her eyes. The walker looked up and smiled.

Rachel lifted her sunglasses and waved to Hannah Bodine, curator of the small Fairhaven Historical Museum that shared space at the Arts Center. Moving N.C.Y.T. there had been Hannah's idea. Maybe she could help smooth things over with Cam, or at least give her some direction. Rachel strolled over and greeted her friend.

"Out for walk and a little fresh air?" Hannah asked.

Rachel shrugged, struggling to summon a smile.

"What's wrong, dear?"

Hannah's kindness and interest in N.C.Y.T. had won Rachel's trust and friendship, so she plunged ahead. "I had a run-in with Cam." Her throat suddenly felt thick, and a weight seemed to press down on her shoulders. "I'm afraid he's going to ask us to leave."

"Oh dear. What happened?"

Rachel related the story, even confessing how she'd spoken her mind a little too freely. "I don't know what it is about that man. I just can't seem to keep a lid on my temper when he's around."

"He seems to have a powerful effect on you." Hannah's eyes twinkled.

"Oh, there's nothing going on between us. I wouldn't even call us friends. Our relationship is more like the explosive reaction you get when you mix vinegar and soda."

Hannah chuckled. "Sounds exciting!"

"Seriously, Hannah. I think I pushed Cam too far today." Why had she unloaded all her frustration on him? If she'd held her tongue, or at least apologized after she'd blown up, things might have worked out differently.

"I wouldn't worry too much. Cam may seem all rough and bristly on the outside, but he has a good heart. He'll cool off."

"I still don't understand why he was so upset. It was just a little noise and a small puddle of water. Why is he so antagonistic toward my kids?"

The amusement faded from Hannah's eyes, and she patted Rachel's arm. "Come on. Let's walk. I want to get in a few more minutes of exercise before the rains come."

"Okay." Rachel set off, matching Hannah's brisk pace.

"Cam has his reasons for being sensitive about children." The older woman's voice softened. "He lost his wife and son a few years ago in a terrible car accident."

Rachel nodded. "He told me."

Hannah's steps slowed. "He did?"

"Yes, I saw their photo at his house."

Hannah cocked her head, a slight smile lifting the corners of her mouth. "He invited you to his house?"

Warning bells rang in Rachel's head. Here was another opportunity to lead someone on with a little bit of truth. But she didn't want to make the same mistake this time. "He did invite me in, but only because I'm renting his upstairs apartment."

Hannah's eyes danced now. "Really?"

"I'm just the tenant. That's all there is to it."

"Okay. If you say so." But Hannah's smile said she suspected a budding romance between her and Cam.

"So you think having my drama kids around reminds Cam of the son he lost?"

"Yes. That's part of it."

"And what's the other part?"

"I think he's afraid of getting involved and risking that kind of loss again. So he puts up this gruff front to keep people at a distance, especially women and children."

Rachel turned that idea over in her mind. It made sense, considering everything she had observed about Cam in the past few weeks. Suddenly her irritation with him seemed trivial, even petty. Regret burned in her throat. How would she cope if she had suffered such a great loss?

"God and time have a way of healing old wounds," Hannah added, sending her a brief smile. "Maybe that's why you're here."

Rachel laughed softly. "I doubt my coming to Fairhaven is going to play a part in Cam's healing. All I seem to do is irritate him."

"Maybe so, but helping him over the hurdle of being with children every day could be an important step forward for him."

Rachel bit her lip, pondering that thought. Could she and her kids really be part of God's plan to help Cam overcome his grief?

"Are you willing to put up with a little fuss and fluster from him?"

Rachel grimaced. "I suppose so. What choice do I have? There's nowhere else for me to go."

Hannah gave her a teasing poke in the side. "Well don't look as if it's going to be such torture. It might turn out to be good for both of you. Cam has his good points."

"Really? Like what?"

"Well…he does a fine job managing his shop and the co-op. He's got a good head for numbers, and he's a skilled craftsman. People come from all over Bellingham and pay top dollar for his framing. But more important than that, he's loyal and caring, and he watches out for all of us." She slipped her arm around Rachel's shoulder and smiled. "He can actually be quite charming when the mood strikes."

"That, I would like to see." As her teasing words faded into the wind, she remembered how he'd helped her move into her apartment. He'd worked all day, carried in more loads than she could count and never once complained. And that night, when they sat in her new kitchen and shared pizza and stories from their lives, she thought they'd truly connected.

A smile tugged at her lips as she recalled how he thought Josh was her live-in boyfriend. His confession had touched a soft place in her heart, and she'd sensed the possibility of a friendship beginning.

But that was last week—before their argument.

Rachel shook her head and released a soft sigh. Why had she been so defensive? Not only had she damaged her chance to gain Cam's support for N.C.Y.T., she'd put another roadblock in the way of them becoming friends.

And that was what bothered her most of all.

Chapter Eight

Cam gripped the hoe and attacked the weeds that had sprung up between the rows of tomatoes and peppers in his garden. Grumbling to himself, he continued whacking away at the nasty intruders while he replayed his quarrel with Rachel.

She was wrong. There was no way around it. She should've kept an eye on those kids even if they weren't her students. He couldn't let that go. It was his responsibility to oversee the Arts Center. If he didn't, his business as well as his friends' would suffer.

But he shouldn't have come on so strong. He didn't need to blow her out of the water just to make his point. Why hadn't he stopped when her face turned ghostly pale and her warm brown eyes hardened to cool slate?

Pitching another weed on the pile, he huffed. If he hadn't been so hardheaded maybe she wouldn't have run away from him with that painful look of betrayal in her eyes.

He'd wounded her with his words, and that was much worse than any damage those kids had done.

Kneeling, he grabbed an obstinate weed and tugged it out of the ground. If only he could uproot his own selfishness and pride. Perhaps then Rachel would care about what he had to say.

Tires crunched on the gravel driveway as a car rolled to a stop on the other side of the tall wooden fence. His stomach took a nosedive. That had to be Rachel. He stood and brushed the dirt from his hands.

The trunk latch released, the car door slammed, and he heard her footsteps. The gate squeaked open. She stepped through carrying four plastic grocery bags, her computer case over her shoulder and a red umbrella clamped under one arm. She turned and gave the gate a kick, slamming it closed.

He strode across the lawn toward her. "Let me give you a hand with those."

She swung around, her eyes wide. "Oh. I didn't see you."

"I was working in the garden."

She looked past his shoulder, obviously avoiding eye contact with him.

"Can I help you carry those upstairs?"

"No thanks." She sent him a cool glance, adjusted her hold on the bags and walked away.

Regret swamped him. "Rachel, wait."

She slowly turned around, the challenge still evident in her eyes.

"I've been thinking about what happened today." He shoved his hands in his jeans' pockets and rocked back on his heels. He hated to admit he was wrong, but that was the only way to straighten this out. "I made a big deal out of something we could've easily worked out with a little discussion."

Her wary expression softened a little. "I didn't exactly make it easy for us to talk it over."

He shrugged. "That's true."

She stared at him for a second. Then she seemed to realize he was teasing. "Okay. I'm ready to listen to whatever you have to say."

A grin tugged at his lips. "Wow. That's all it took?"

"Well, that and a talk with Hannah on the Taylor Avenue dock."

He cocked his head. "What?"

"Never mind. It's not important." She set down the bags. "I've been thinking about it, too. And I'm sorry I was so defensive, but I felt…"

"Attacked?"

"Yes."

"I guess I did come on a little strong."

She lifted her brows, sending him a meaningful look.

"Well, I suppose I was more like a bulldozer at a construction site."

"A little." The light returned to her eyes.

"Do you want to sit down?" He motioned toward the round table and four chairs shaded by a large green umbrella. "Maybe we could talk for a while."

She hesitated and glanced across the patio. "Okay. But I need to run upstairs and put some ice cream in the freezer." She bent down to grab her bags.

"Whoa, did you say ice cream?"

She looked up and nodded.

He peaked in one of her bags. "What flavor?"

"Moose tracks."

"Wow. That sounds good. What do I have to do to convince you to share?"

"Hmm." She tapped her chin for a moment, then her teasing expression faded. "How about promising you'll give me another chance?" The sincerity in her eyes was unmistakable.

He nodded. "If you'll do the same for me."

Sunday afternoon Cam followed Ross through the crowd gathered in Fairhaven's historic district. The number of people packed into the eight-block area for this year's festival was definitely higher than last year.

The sun shone down, warming Cam's shoulders and lifting his mood. He didn't normally like crowds, but this one seemed focused on enjoying the day, so he didn't mind mixing with them. Live music from a band on the Village Green stage filled in the air with a lively, upbeat sound. The mouthwatering scent of grilling meat floated past, teasing his nose.

Earlier that day, he and Ross had watched several kayakers race to the shore, run up the hill and ring the bell, signaling the end of their team's efforts to make it from the top of Mt. Baker to Bellingham Bay in the annual Ski to Sea Race.

The community festival, celebrating the end of the race and the beginning of summer, was a favorite with people from all over the Bellingham area. As Cam made his way through the Memorial Day weekend crowd, he agreed it was worth the hassle of finding a place to park and feeling like a fish swimming upstream against the flow.

"Why didn't we sign up for a booth?" Ross pointed to the line of tents filled with all types of artwork. "We could've all gone in together and put up a great display."

"File that idea away for next year." Another whiff of something barbequed floated past. Cam's mouth watered, and he glanced at his watch. "Let's grab something to eat."

"Okay. Just a minute." Ross lifted his camera, adjusted the settings and snapped another photo. "Maybe I can sell some of these to *Entertainment News NW* or the *Bellingham Herald*."

"Don't they send their own photographers to big events like this?"

"Sure, but if I get a great shot…" He clicked off another series of photos. "…maybe they'll buy it."

Cam nodded, though Ross was still viewing the festival through his camera lens.

"Hey, there's a great subject." Ross grinned and continued clicking away.

Cam glanced across the street in the direction Ross had pointed his camera. Rachel and another young woman with long red hair stood in front of a booth displaying used books, movie posters and records.

Cam blew out a deep breath and frowned at the sidewalk.

Ross glanced at him. "What's the matter?"

"Nothing." Cam folded his arms across his chest and looked back toward the Village Green.

"I thought you worked things out with Rachel."

Cam's face grew hot. "I did." He hated that Ross could read him so easily.

"So what's with the face?"

"I just feel a little weird around her, that's all."

Ross cocked his head. "How come?"

He shrugged, feeling like an awkward adolescent instead of a thirty-three-year-old man.

"Well, I think Rachel's one of the nicest people I've met in a long time. And she's certainly easy on the eyes." Ross glanced at Cam as he adjusted the strap on his camera. "In fact, I've been thinking about asking her out."

Cam pulled back. "No way. You're not."

"Yeah. I am." Grinning, Ross pushed his dark frame glasses up his thin nose.

"But…she's not your type," he sputtered.

"Sure she is. We're both fun-loving and creative. I think we have a lot in common."

Cam shook his head. "You're too young for her."

Ross laughed. "I'm twenty-seven. She can't be much older than that. And a few years age difference doesn't bother me." He wiggled his dark brows. "Besides, older women have more experience, and that's a plus in my book."

Cam clenched his jaw. "You better watch it."

Ross's grin hitched up higher. "Ha! I knew it. You like her."

"No!" Cam wanted to kick himself. He'd walked right into that one.

"Come on, Cam. You don't have to pretend with me."

"Look, I wish you'd drop this."

"If you like her, you should ask her out."

"No. I'm not ready to date Rachel or anyone else."

Understanding glimmered in Ross's eyes, and his mischievous expression faded. "It's been four years, Cam. It's okay to be attracted to someone else."

Cam's throat constricted. Four years wasn't long

enough to erase the painful memories. He'd never realized how much his wife and son meant to him until it was too late and they were gone.

"Your wife wouldn't expect you to mourn forever," Ross added. "She'd want to you to move on and make the most of your life."

Cam swallowed and tried to find his voice. "You didn't even know Marie."

Ross nodded, his expression sober. "You're right. I didn't. But I know you. And I think it's time you stop punishing yourself for what happened. It's not going to bring Marie back."

Cam turned away and pulled in a shaky breath. Ross was right. There was nothing Cam could do to bring his wife and son back. Marie and Tyler were gone forever because he'd been too self-absorbed to protect them the way a husband and father should.

He could never forgive himself for that.

Chapter Nine

Rachel flipped through the display of old movie posters and spotted one featuring Fred Astaire and Ginger Rogers dancing cheek-to-cheek. She smiled and pulled it from the rack. "Look at this."

Chandra Wetzel, her friend and choreographer for N.C.Y.T. walked over for a better view. "Oh, I love Fred Astaire. What a charmer." Sunlight glinted off Chandra's red wavy hair. Her white peasant blouse and flowing blue skirt showed off her dancer's figure and reflected her free-spirited style. Chandra sighed with a wistful smile. "Nobody dances like that anymore."

"They've got some great movie posters." Rachel turned back toward the rack and began thumbing through. "Maybe I should buy a few for the classrooms. What do you think?" When Chandra didn't answer, Rachel glanced up at her friend.

"Someone is watching us," Chandra gave a subtle nod as she looked past Rachel's shoulder.

"What do you mean?"

"There's a guy across the street taking our picture."

Fear snaked up Rachel's back and tightened around her chest, making it hard to pull in her next breath. Could it be Kyle? Had he followed her all the way up here from Seattle? How was that possible? She thought she'd covered her tracks by changing jobs, changing phone numbers and moving more than ninety miles away. "Is he tall with dark hair?" Rachel forced out the words, refusing to turn around and see for herself.

"Yeah, and he's kind of cute in a quirky way. Nice dresser." Chandra smiled and started to lift her hand.

Panic skittered along Rachel's nerves. "Wait!" She grabbed Chandra's arm. "I don't want him to know we see him."

"It's too late for that. I already smiled at him." Chandra frowned at her. "What's the matter?"

"I…I just don't like the idea of someone taking my picture without my permission." With a shaky hand she replaced the poster. Should she slip out the other side of the tent and hope he wouldn't follow, or turn around and face him?

Confronting Kyle had only made things worse in Seattle. The police advised her to ignore him and pretend his skulking around didn't bother her. But that had been impossible.

What if he started following her again? A cold sweat broke out on her forehead, and her stomach swirled. She touched Chandra's shoulder. "Let's get out of here."

"But I thought you wanted to get some posters."

"Not now. We need to leave." Rachel wove through the display of books, heading toward the opposite side of the tent.

"The guy's not creepy or anything. He looks totally normal."

Rachel shook her head. That's what she'd thought at first, too. It was only later she learned Kyle's problems were well hidden behind his winsome appearance. "It's not normal to spy on someone with a camera." She ducked out the back door of the tent. "Come on. Let's cut across the Village Green."

Chandra followed, toting two shopping bags of items she'd purchased earlier. "I don't think he was spying on us. He's probably just a photographer from the paper or something. He had a nice camera, and there was another guy with him who looked like a reporter—blond curly hair, good-looking, but he had kind of a fierce expression."

Rachel turned. "What did you say?"

"I'm saying we just walked away from two cute guys who probably wanted to meet us, and that's a cryin' shame."

"No, I mean about the guy with the photographer."

Chandra shrugged. "I said he's blond and good-looking, sort of reminded me of a lion."

Rachel gulped in a breath.

"Rachel?" a man called from somewhere behind her.

She stopped, her heart pounding in her throat, trying to process the voice. It didn't sound like Kyle, but—

Chandra spun around. "Hey, the photographer knows you?"

Rachel swallowed and slowly turned around.

Ross and Cam wove through the crowded Village Green toward them. Cam sent her a half smile. Ross lifted his hand and waved.

"Well, if it isn't our mystery men," Chandra whispered.

Rachel's heartbeat slowly returned to normal, and she forced a smile. "Hi, guys."

Rachel introduced Chandra. "She's the choreographer for N.C.Y.T., so you'll be seeing a lot more of her around the Arts Center soon."

"Wow, that's great. I'm a bit of a dancer myself." Ross did a brief tap dance right there on the brick walkway.

Chandra grinned. "You could give Fred Astaire a run for his money."

"If he was still alive," Cam added with a wry smile.

Ross ignored Cam. "So, have you lovely ladies had lunch?"

"Not yet." Chandra smiled, her blue eyes shining.

"Cam and I were just headed over to get something to eat. Would you like to come along?"

Rachel glanced at Cam, trying to gauge how he felt about the invitation, but he remained silent and unreadable. Chandra watched her expectantly. "Sure. We're ready for lunch."

"I wish we hadn't parked so far away." Chandra held up her two shopping bags. "I'd love to stash these. My arms are getting tired."

"My car is just around the corner. Why don't you and I walk up there and put these in the trunk?" Ross reached for one of Chandra's bags. "Maybe you two could scout out the lunch options, and we'll meet you back here in about ten minutes."

Cam nodded. "Sure."

Rachel fell into step beside Cam. An awkward silence settled around them as they followed the smell of grilled burgers drifting in the air. "Did you and Ross see the craft booths?"

Cam nodded. "We should probably sign up next year."

"Good idea." She smiled, glad he'd come to that conclusion himself.

"So, drama classes start next week?" He didn't look too bothered by the prospect. That was a good sign.

"Yes, on Tuesday. I can't wait for the kids to see our new classrooms and the auditorium. There's so much more space, such potential. They're going to love it!"

A smile lifted one side of his mouth. "You are the eternal optimist."

She ducked her chin and laughed. "I suppose so. Hope it's not too irritating."

His gaze connected with hers. "I'm getting used to it."

A zing of awareness traveled through her, and her heart lifted.

His cell phone rang. He pulled it from his pocket and looked at the screen. "It's my sister, Shannon." He sent her an apologetic look. "I should probably take this."

"Oh, sure. I don't mind." They stopped in the shade of a tree in front of a cute shop called Katie's Cupcakes. Rachel turned to look at a display of delicious looking bakery items that had been set out on tables along the sidewalk.

Cam tapped the screen and lifted the cell phone to his ear. "Hi, Shannon. What's up?"

Rachel took a couple steps away, giving him a bit of privacy, but she was still close enough to hear his side of the conversation.

"What?" His face darkened, and his golden brows drew together. "When did you find out?" He turned and paced down the sidewalk a few steps. "Are you sure about this place? What does Eric say? Maybe I should check it out." He listened for a couple more minutes, his profile stern.

"What about Kayla?" Cam's lips formed a grim line. "Sure. Whatever you need. I'll see what I can find out and call you tonight." He tapped the screen to end his call and dropped the phone in his pocket.

"Everything okay?" Rachel asked.

An unsettled look filled his eyes. "My sister had cancer a few years ago, and it's back."

Rachel's stomach dropped. "Oh, Cam. I'm sorry."

"Me, too. She had surgery and chemo treatments four years ago. That was really rough on her, but she made it through, and every test has been clear until now."

Rachel folded her arms, hugging them across her stomach. "What will she do now?"

"She wants to go to a special treatment center in Mexico. I'm going to check it out online, maybe give them a call. I don't really like the idea of her going out of the country, but she seems to think it's the best option." He rubbed his neck and blew out a deep breath.

"Is she married?"

"Yes. Her husband, Eric, is a great guy. If she goes to Mexico, he'll go with her, and they want me to take care of their daughter, Kayla." Uncertainty filled his eyes. "I'll do anything I can to help them… but I'm not sure how I'd keep a fourteen-year-old girl busy all summer."

"She'd need to stay that long?"

He nodded. "Eight to twelve weeks. The program includes medical treatment, nutrition, counseling and emotional and spiritual support."

Her ears perked up at the mention of spiritual support. What did he mean by that?

They started off down the sidewalk at a slower pace. Rachel couldn't imagine how difficult it would be to face cancer the second time, or to watch your mom fight that kind of battle. Remembering the girls in her drama group and all the normal emotional ups and downs at that age, her heart went out to Kayla. This had to be a huge challenge for her, for all of them.

But just feeling sympathetic wasn't going to change anything. True compassion meant reaching out to help. But what could she do?

An idea began to take shape in her mind, and she looked up at Cam. "Do you think Kayla would like to come to drama camp?"

"I don't know." He pondered it a moment, then shook his head. "I don't think we can afford that right now. Paying for Shannon's cancer treatment has to be the priority for all of us."

Rachel nodded. "I'd like to offer her a scholarship. She could come as many days a week as you like for as long as she's here. Maybe she'd like to try out for the summer musical. That would really keep her busy. And she'd be right there in the building with you all day."

The lines on his forehead eased. "Wow, that's quite an offer."

"She'd spend time with kids her own age and learn some new skills."

He smiled. "Thanks, Rachel. I appreciate it, and I know Kayla will, too." His warm expression totally changed his face.

"I wish I could do more. I can't imagine going through something like this at her age."

"Yeah, it's been hard on all of them for the last few years, especially waiting and wondering after each checkup. And now Shannon is facing an even bigger battle." He clenched his jaw and looked away, but not quick enough to hide the moisture glistening in his eyes.

Rachel touched his arm. "I'll pray for her, Cam, for all of you."

"Thanks. I know that's how she made it through the first time. Hundreds of people prayed for her. She and Eric are both Christians…. I just hope their faith is strong enough for what's ahead."

Cam talked about his family's faith in such familiar terms, but where did he stand?

A tremor passed through her. "What about you, Cam? How are you going to get through this?"

He narrowed his eyes and focused on the crowd passing by. "Guess I'm going to do what I always do. Stay focused, keep working, hope for the best, but prepare for the worst."

Her heart sunk like a rock tossed in a pond. How could that kind of belief system help him through a huge trial like this? Why didn't he tap into the hope and spiritual anchor God longed to provide?

Chapter Ten

Bright morning sunlight filtered through the tall windows on the side of the Arts Center auditorium. Rachel stood by the first row of chairs with her eyes trained on Amy Buchanan.

Her college-age intern led a group of young drama camp students up the steps to the stage. After assisting Rachel and Chandra for four days, Amy had reluctantly agreed to lead a group by herself. But she had begged Rachel to stay for a few minutes and be sure she got off to a good start. That made sense. These kids had a lot of energy, especially this younger group.

"Okay. Let's have everyone sit in a semi-circle." Amy's soft voice could barely be heard over the kid's conversations.

"Hey, everyone, listen up!" Rachel clapped her hands, and the kids immediately settled down. She forced a smile and motioned for Amy to continue.

"We're going to do a fun activity called Story, Story." Amy's gentle voice quivered as the students filed across the stage.

Rachel held her breath. This had to work.

"Okay. Sarah, you're first. Come up here in the acting area." Amy motioned the petite ten-year-old to join her at center stage. "Jeff, you're going to tell a story, and Sarah will to act it out as you tell it in whatever way seems best to her."

Rachel's stomach tightened. Amy needed to speak up and take charge or the kids were going to run all over her. *Please, Lord, help her figure it out.*

They'd almost made it through the first week of drama camp. But it had been a rough start with a new location, a new intern and several new younger students. Keeping the kids quiet while they changed classes was a constant struggle. So far, she'd managed not to upset any of her co-op partners.

Her thoughts drifted to Cam, as they did more often lately. Since they'd talked about his sister at the festival, they seemed more comfortable around each other, less like enemies and a bit more like friends. That thought made her smile. But her smile faded as she thought of the spiritual chasm that seemed to separate them.

Chandra strolled down the aisle to meet Rachel. She leaned closer. "How's Amy doing?"

"Not too well," Rachel whispered. "I hope she's got what it takes."

"She better, or we're in deep trouble. Twenty-five students is too many for one group, especially with the age spread."

"You're right. We need three groups, but I can't afford to hire anyone else. It's Amy or nothing."

"Then we'll just have to keep praying and coach her along."

Rachel nodded. "That's the plan."

Chandra shifted her gaze toward the back of the auditorium, and her eyes widened. "Uh-oh, here comes trouble."

Rachel tensed and turned around. Cam walked toward them wearing a stern expression.

"I better scoot and check on my group. I left Ryan in charge." Chandra headed up the opposite aisle, cutting a wide path around Cam.

He headed straight for Rachel. As he came closer she noticed the sag of his shoulders and the troubled look in his blue-gray eyes.

"Can we talk for a minute?"

"Sure." She glanced at Amy, shot off another prayer, then followed him out into the hallway.

He turned and faced her. "Shannon called this morning. The arrangements are all made. My niece arrives Saturday." He looked at her as though she ought to understand why that was such distressing news.

"Next Saturday?"

"No. Tomorrow night."

"Oh…. Are you ready?"

He blew out a deep breath and rubbed the back of his neck. "That's what I wanted to talk to you about. All I have in my guest bedroom is a twin bed and a dresser. I have no idea what a fourteen-year-old girl needs, so I was wondering if you had time to take a look and give me some suggestions."

"Sure. I could do that."

"Thank you." He looked so relieved she thought he might hug her, but he didn't. "When are you done today?"

"Camp is over at noon. I just have a few things to finish up in my office after that. I could be back at the house around one. Would that work for you?"

"I have a couple people coming in this morning, but I'm sure I'll be done by then." He sent her a grateful smile. "Thanks, Rachel. I really appreciate this." Then he headed back to his shop.

Rachel grinned and did a little dance step as she walked back to the auditorium. So, he needed some feminine input and decorating advice. No problem. She'd be glad to help. This was a great opportunity for her to strengthen their relationship. And if she and Cam became good friends, N.C.Y.T. would be assured of a permanent home at the Arts Center.

But she'd have to be careful and not let her emotions lead her down the wrong path. Cam didn't seem to have a personal faith in God, and that was a non-negotiable on her list.

* * *

Cam shifted his weight and tried to look interested as Hannah Bodine continued describing several more old family photos she planned to bring in for framing.

"I hope you'll be able to find more of that sepia mat board. That's the perfect color. I'd like these other photos to match the first one you framed for me."

He nodded. "I have it on order."

"Good." She smiled as she looked at the photos she had come to pick up. "I'm so pleased with what you've done. This will look lovely in my dining room, although Arthur said he'd rather hang it in the entryway."

Cam glanced at the clock on the wall above Hannah's head, and silently tapped his foot on the floor. Twelve forty-five. He didn't want to be rude and rush Hannah out the door, but he didn't want to keep Rachel waiting. With only a little more than twenty-four hours to spruce up the guestroom, he didn't have time to waste.

"So, what do you think?" Hannah tilted her head, waiting for his answer.

"Oh, sorry, I missed what you said."

The older woman chuckled. "It's all right. I was just asking if I could bring the rest of the photos in Monday morning around ten."

"That's fine. I'll write it on the calendar." He

moved to his desk and jotted the appointment down, hoping that would signal the end of their conversation.

He turned around just as Rachel walked past outside his window headed toward the parking lot. Her car sat with seven others in the row closest to the building. The rest of the parking lot looked empty except for one car sitting in the far corner in the shade of several tall trees.

His senses sharpened. The night he'd walked Rachel to her car after the co-op meeting they'd spotted a dark sedan parked there. He would've forgotten all about it if Rachel hadn't been so shaken by it. He didn't want to say anything to her, but he'd seen a similar car parked there a few other times since then.

"Well, I'm off. I have to stop in at Village Books, then I'm going on to my daughter's to see my darling grandson." Hannah picked up the framed photos. "Bye, Cam. Have a nice weekend."

"Thanks, Hannah." Cam crossed to the window and scanned the parking lot. Rachel opened her back passenger door and placed her purse and computer case inside, then she closed the door and climbed in the driver's seat.

Across the parking lot, the driver of the black car flicked a cigarette out the window. The dark-tinted car window rose, hiding him from view.

Cam's heartbeat kicked up a notch.

Rachel backed out of her parking spot and drove toward the exit. When she turned right onto the street, the car in the corner slowly pulled out and followed her.

The hair on the back of Cam's neck stood on end. He turned, grabbed his keys and phone from the desk and dashed out the door. It might be just a weird coincidence, but if someone was following Rachel, he intended to find out and put a stop to it.

Rachel hummed along with a praise song on the radio as she pulled into the driveway at Cam's house. As she reached to turn off the engine, her car door swung open.

Cam leaned down and looked in. "Are you okay?"

"Yes. I'm fine."

He looked toward the street, and then back at her, concern darkening his eyes.

"What's going on?" She followed his gaze, but she didn't see anything unusual.

He hesitated and finally gave a half shrug. "You left the Arts Center before me. So when I pulled in and you weren't here, I was worried."

"I stopped at the bank." That didn't ease the lines from his forehead. "What is it?"

He looked down and wiped his hand on his pants. "Nothing." Yet he still looked guarded as he opened her car door the rest of the way and watched her climb out. "You ready to go see Kayla's room?"

"Sure." She gathered her purse and computer bag from the backseat, pondering Cam's strange welcome. She appreciated his concern, but it seemed odd for him to be anxious when she was only a few minutes late.

She followed him inside. He greeted his dog, Sasha, then led Rachel down the hall to the spare bedroom. "This is it."

Rachel stepped through the doorway, and her questions about Cam's odd behavior faded from her mind. This sparse little room definitely needed a facelift. The white walls, ceiling and woodwork reminded her of a hospital room. A simple maple-framed twin bed was pushed against one wall. A matching four-drawer dresser in the corner was the only other piece of furniture.

"It's pretty bad isn't it?"

"Well, let's just say there's lots of room for improve-ment."

"Right. The old cup-half-full approach." He cocked his head and grinned.

"Yes." She smiled. "Do those need to stay?" She pointed to a stack of five cardboard boxes lined up against one wall.

"Yeah. I used to store them in the basement, but I've had a little water down there this spring. I need to keep them up here for now."

"Okay. We can work with that." She crossed the room counting her footsteps. The floor was bare but beautiful hardwood. "So it looks like it's about twelve by eighteen."

He looked around. "There's plenty of space, it just looks a little like a jail cell." He stuffed his hands in his pockets. "What do you think I ought to do?"

She pulled a small notebook from her purse. "Let's draw a floor plan. Do you have a tape measure?"

"Sure." He left to retrieve one, while she noted the placement of the windows, door and closet on her drawing.

Cam returned, and they took several measurements.

Rachel jotted the numbers in her notebook. "The first thing on the list is picking out a comforter set. That will help you choose a color scheme. Then you'll need curtains, blinds, sheets, maybe a throw rug and a few things for the wall." Her enthusiasm built as she began to picture the transformed room. "We could start at the bed and bath store at the mall. I've got some twenty percent off coupons. Then I know this great little thrift shop where we might find some used furniture, maybe a desk or bookshelf."

Cam's face lit up. "Did you say, *we?*"

"Yes." She grinned. "I'm not going to abandon you to do all this on your own."

He clasped his hands and lifted his eyes toward the ceiling. "Thank you."

She chuckled, determined to help him, whether he was teasing about the prayer or not. "We'll make this into a beautiful room Kayla will love. And I promise it'll be done in twenty-four hours, and it won't break your bank account."

"Wow, talk about an extreme home makeover, sounds like you just might give that TV show a run for their money."

With her laughter bubbling over and a silent prayer in her heart, she followed him out the door.

Rachel fastened her seatbelt and glanced at the remarkable pile of treasure stashed in the back of Cam's SUV. In a little under four hours they'd found a beautiful aqua, lime and lavender comforter set with matching curtains, a cute area rug, a white wicker nightstand and rocker, a lamp with a shell fringe shade, and a funky wicker trunk—and all for under three hundred dollars.

"You're quite the bargain hunter." Cam gazed at the road ahead, a slight smile lifting the corners of his mouth. "I had no idea there were such great deals at thrift shops." He took the freeway entrance and headed south toward Fairhaven. "It's wild the way we found everything we needed, and it all looks like it goes together."

"Pretty amazing." The afternoon had been quite an adventure as they compared prices at the store and then sorted through all the crazy castoffs at the resale shops. She'd seen a more relaxed side of Cam today, and she found it very appealing.

She shifted in her seat to look at him. "I am a pretty good shopper, but I don't deserve all the credit."

He lifted his brows and grinned. "Don't tell me you had a secret shopper out there scouting out bargains for us."

"Not exactly. But I did pray and asked God for help before we left."

He considered that for a moment. "Well, looks like He answered your prayer."

Her heart lifted. That was a positive response, wasn't it? She studied Cam's handsome profile—his square jaw, straight Roman nose and high forehead topped with blond curls. He did have a strong personality, but he wasn't nearly as fearsome as she'd first believed. Underneath his gruff exterior there was humor and compassion along with a host of other good qualities he was just beginning to let her see.

"It's almost six. Do you want to stop and get something to eat?" he asked.

Rachel's empty stomach twisted, but should she turn this shopping trip into a date? What if she offered to pay for her own meal? Would it still be considered a date? Oh brother, she was probably making too much of this. Why not stop and have dinner together? They were both hungry. It made sense…but would that be leading him on?

Rachel stifled a groan. Why did she feel so clueless when it came to making a decision about men and relationships? Never having her father around as she was growing up probably had more to do with it than she liked to admit. But knowing his absence left a huge hole in her heart didn't help solve her problems with men.

Cam glanced her way. "It's okay if you'd rather not. I just thought you might be hungry."

"No…I mean, yes." She pushed away her doubts. "Dinner sounds great."

His face brightened. "Okay. What kind of food do you like?"

She suggested the Colophone Café back in Fairhaven. It offered delicious soups, salads and sandwiches in a casual setting. He agreed, and they found a parking place nearby.

A cool breeze blew up the hill from Bellingham Bay carrying the scent of the ocean as Rachel and Cam walked toward the café.

"So, how long have you lived in Fairhaven?" she asked.

"I grew up in Bellingham, just north of here. Went to Western Washington University." He chuckled and shook his head. "The first couple years I majored in fun and games, so it took me five years to get my finance degree."

She grinned at his confession. "I see."

"Then my dad passed away when I was twenty. That ended all the partying for me."

"I'm sorry. I didn't know you'd lost your dad."

"Yeah. It was a tough time. But it made me wake up and make some decisions about how I was going to live the rest of my life."

She wondered what he meant, but he didn't say more. "Is your mom still alive?"

"Yes. She is in her mid-sixties and is still going strong. She does a lot of volunteer work and walks every day." They reached the café, and he held the door open for her. They sat at a table overlooking the Village Green.

"How about you?" Cam asked. "Where did you grow up?"

"I was born in Chicago, but my parents divorced when I was two, and Mom and I moved out to Seattle to be near my grandparents." The server arrived and gave them menus.

"So, are your parents still living?"

"Mom's in Seattle." She hesitated. Her parents' issues weren't her fault, but for some reason she always felt guilty whenever she talked about them. "I'm…not sure about my dad."

Cam looked up from his menu.

She swallowed and forced herself to go on. "He had a drinking problem and he made life miserable for my mom. Things got so bad she decided to leave."

Cam frowned. "So, do you have contact with him now?"

"No. I never have. Mom was afraid he'd follow us, so she changed our names and kept a low profile."

He studied her a moment longer, his gaze softening. "That must've been hard growing up without a dad."

"Knowing I had a father I had to hide from was even harder." She looked away and clutched her napkin in her lap. Why had she said that? Ever since she was a little girl, her mom had warned her to keep that information to herself. How many times had she heard her mother say, *Don't hang your dirty laundry in public?*

Thankfully, the waitress returned to the their table. Rachel ordered the first sandwich on the list—a turkey wrap with fresh fruit. Cam asked for a steak sandwich with fries and coleslaw.

Time to change the subject before he asked her any more questions about her father. "How did you get into framing when you graduated with a finance degree?"

"I started out working for a large investment company, moved up quickly, and was making a good salary, but I was putting in more than sixty hours a week. Definitely not a good thing for a man with a family."

"So you changed careers to have more time with them?"

He shook his head, unmistakable sorrow lining his face. "I wish that was true." He took a sip of his iced tea. "I didn't change jobs until after the accident. I couldn't go back to my old way of life. It all seemed so pointless. Finally, my uncle Ken hauled me down to his frame shop and put me to work. He told me if I kept my hands busy it might help me work through everything."

"He taught you about framing?"

"Yes, and he probably saved my life in the process."

His words settled over her heart, bringing new compassion and clarity. No wonder he struggled to see the cup half full. He'd lost his father, wife and son in a few short years, and now he faced losing his sister as well. She started to reach for his hand, but the waitress returned, bringing them their meals.

He cleared his throat. "Sorry, that was a little heavy for dinner conversation."

"No. I'm glad you told me." She looked down at her plate. "Would you mind if I prayed?"

"No, go ahead." He bowed his head.

She closed her eyes. "Thank You, Father, for this meal and for helping us find so many great things for Kayla's room. Please watch over Shannon and Eric as they travel to Mexico. We ask for Your healing hand to be on Shannon, and we pray for Kayla, too. Amen."

"Thanks." Cam smiled at her across the table. They ate in silence for a few minutes, then he asked, "So did you go to college in Seattle?"

"Yes, Seattle Pacific. I majored in theater with a teaching emphasis."

"Did you move up here to teach after graduation?"

She took a bite and chewed slowly. Her situation was complicated, but she didn't want to mislead him. "I taught in Seattle for six years. But for the last three summers I came up to Bellingham and worked as assistant director of N.C.Y.T."

He cocked his head. "So how long have you been the director?"

"Since January. I took over for my friend Suzanne. She and Josh are having a baby, and it was the right time for me to make a move."

Cam's eyes widened as he looked past Rachel's shoulder. "Oh no," he muttered and ducked his head.

Rachel turned and looked across the café.

Melanie walked toward their table followed by Lilly. "Well, this is certainly a surprise. What are you two doing here?"

Rachel sucked in a breath and almost choked on her sandwich.

"We're having dinner." Cam's tone was cool and even.

"I can see that."

A nervous laugh escaped Lilly's mouth. "We just had dinner, too."

An awkward silence settled around them. Someone had to say something. "Cam's niece is arriving tomorrow, so we were out shopping for some things to fix up her room," Rachel said.

Melanie's eyes flashed. "Shannon's daughter?" Cam nodded. She hiked her purse higher on her shoulder. "How long is she staying?"

"I'm not sure."

Apparently Cam hadn't told Melanie or Lilly his sister had cancer again, or that he'd be caring for his niece this summer.

"Well, bring her by the shop, and I'll let her design a piece of jewelry while she's here."

"Okay." Cam's answer didn't carry much enthusiasm.

Lilly laid her hand on Melanie's arm. "Well, Mel and I are on our way to do a little shopping. We'll see you later."

Melanie shot them one last heated glance then strutted out of the café with Lilly.

Cam focused on his plate and took another bite of his sandwich. His face definitely looked a shade or two darker than it had earlier.

Rachel suppressed a smile, but a giggle worked

its way up her throat. She lifted her hand to stifle the sound, but it was too late.

Cam looked up. "What's so funny?"

"Sorry. I was thinking about the way Melanie's eyes just about bulged out of their sockets when she saw us sitting here."

He gave in with a grin, which soon turned into a chuckle. "I don't know why, but she doesn't want to let go of the idea that we ought to be more than friends."

Rachel couldn't resist pushing him just a little further. "So, you two aren't dating?"

"No!" He shook his head and actually looked pained by the idea. "Definitely not."

Rachel smiled. "That's…good to know."

Cam led Shannon and Kayla down the hall, then pushed open the door to Kayla's room. "Here you go." He stepped back so his sister and niece could enter.

Kayla stood in the doorway, silently staring straight ahead. Her pinched expression and mottled skin made it clear she'd been crying on the drive from Seattle.

When she didn't speak up, Shannon placed her hand on her daughter's shoulder. "It's lovely, Cam. Such pretty colors. Isn't it great, Kayla?" The forced brightness in Shannon's voice didn't fool either of them.

His niece nodded, but she looked about as happy as a patient waiting for a root canal.

Shannon squeezed her arm. "Come on, now. This is a great room, and your uncle went out of his way to make it special for you." She nodded to her daughter, silently urging her to speak up.

"Thanks, Uncle Cam," Kayla mumbled, then walked over to the bed and trailed her hand over the puffy comforter.

"Really, Cam, you outdid yourself. Everything looks so pulled together." Shannon chuckled. "Sorry, I'm just surprised. Did you watch a home decorating show or something?"

"My upstairs tenant helped me pick everything out. She's got great taste." He smiled, remembering how Rachel had scouted out the best bargains and matched up all the furniture and accessories. Then she'd spent this morning, helping him arrange furniture and hang curtains.

"She?" Shannon's brows rose, and she sent him a questioning smile.

"Yes. She runs the kids' drama program at the Arts Center."

Shannon nodded and sent him a knowing smile.

"Don't give me that look. We're just friends."

Shannon held up her hand. "Okay. I'm just glad to hear you have a friend."

He huffed and glared at her. "Thanks."

Shannon winked. Then she glanced at her watch,

and worry lines gathered around her eyes again. "I've got to go, Kayla." She crossed the room and stood next to her daughter. "Dad and I are meeting with our small group for prayer tonight, then we leave first thing tomorrow morning." She gathered Kayla in a tight hug. Closing her eyes, she rocked back and forth. "I love you, baby girl. Promise me you won't forget that."

Kayla sniffed. "I promise." She clutched her mom and pressed her face against Shannon's shoulder.

When Shannon stepped back, tears glistened in her eyes. "You be good, and have some fun this summer." She lifted her daughter's trembling chin. "Don't worry, sweetie. Everything's going to be fine."

Kayla grabbed her mother in a tight embrace once more as tears coursed down her cheeks.

Cam swallowed hard and clenched his jaw. What made him think he could handle a situation like this? How would he comfort Kayla and help her deal with all the emotions she was feeling? How would he answer her questions? How could he explain why terrible things like this happened to a wonderful woman like Shannon?

Rachel took a fortifying gulp of her French vanilla coffee and motioned Chandra over to the classroom doorway. "Could you take my group for a few minutes. I need to make a phone call."

"Sure. Everything okay?"

"I'm having a hard time straightening out my bill with the storage company. They want to charge me for June, even though I moved everything out by the end of last month. I was hoping if I called them first thing this morning, I might catch someone in a better mood."

Chandra sent her a sympathetic smile. "I'll pray for you."

"Thanks. I need it. It's not a huge amount of money, but right now, it's the difference between eating real food or macaroni and cheese for the rest of the month."

Chandra squeezed Rachel's shoulder. "Let me know how it goes. And remember, my fridge is your fridge. Come over any time."

"Thanks. I may take you up on that." Rachel sent her friend a grateful smile.

Chandra walked to the front of the classroom. "Morning everyone. Time to settle down and get started. We've got a lot planned today, but first I want to remind you about the auditions for our summer musical on Saturday morning. We'll be doing *Anne of Green Gables.*" She took a stack of papers from the desk and sent them around the room. "Auditions start at 9:00 a.m., so read all the info, and be sure to take this sheet home to your parents."

"Ms. Wetzel?" Ten-year-old Gabriel waved his

hand to get her attention. "That sounds like a girl's story. Are there any parts for guys?"

"Yes, Gabe. There are twelve parts for guys and fifteen for girls. Plus we'll need lots of help on the stage crew, so there's something for everyone who'd like to be involved."

Gabe grinned and nodded, looking pleased.

Chandra rounded up the ten youngest students and sent them with Amy. Rachel shot off a silent prayer, asking the Lord to give the timid girl courage.

"I'd like the rest of you to come with me to the auditorium." Chandra lifted her finger and waited. "And remember, we need to be quiet in the hallway."

"We know the drill, Ms. Wetzel—keep a lid on it, or else!" Steve's perfect imitation of Rachel's daily mantra made them all laugh.

"Okay. Glad you got the memo. I don't expect to hear a sound until we're settled in the auditorium."

The chattering faded as they walked out of the classroom, leaving Rachel alone to make her call. She pressed in the number to the storage company. *Lord, please help me reach the right person. You know I can't afford to waste this money.* But she got an answering machine—again. With a sigh, she pressed the off button and slipped her phone in her pocket. She'd have to try again later.

"Rachel?"

She turned as Cam approached her classroom doorway.

Uneasy lines creased his forehead, but he looked as handsome as ever. "Do you have a minute?"

A shiver raced up her back. "Sure. Come on in."

He shuffled over to the desk. "Kayla has barely spoken since her mother dropped her off. She spent most of yesterday shut up in her room. And this morning she announced she was not going anywhere—especially drama camp."

Rachel's stomach dropped. "So what did you say?"

"I told her staying home wasn't an option." He crossed his arms. "I don't get it. Shannon said she liked the idea of going to drama camp. Why would she change her mind now that she's here?"

"She's probably just upset about her mom."

"I'm sure she is, but I can't let her sit home alone all summer."

"So did you talk to her?"

"What's there to talk about? She said she won't go. I told her she either goes to camp or she has to sit in the shop with me all day. She can't stay home."

"How did that go over?"

"Not too well."

"I can imagine. So where is she now?"

He glanced toward the door. "In the shop, sitting on a stool, looking like the world is coming to an end."

"Poor kid. She must be really miserable."

He cocked his head and sent her a confused look.

"Try to see it from her perspective, Cam. She's probably frightened about her mom being sick. She might feel abandoned by her parents. But she can't get mad at them, so she's focusing her anger on you."

His shoulders sagged. "I'm sure you're right. But I don't know how to help her." He lifted his gaze to meet Rachel's. "Would you talk to her?"

The S.O.S. flashing from his blue eyes grabbed her heart and she nodded. "Okay. I'll try."

He released a deep breath. "Thanks. I really appreciate it."

A flash of blue in the hallway caught Rachel's attention.

A young girl with long curly blond hair, large blue eyes and a slim figure looked in the door. This had to be Kayla. The family resemblance was clear in the shape of her chin and high forehead as well as her hair and eye color.

Cam froze, and Rachel could easily read the silent question running through his mind—how much of their conversation had Kayla heard?

Tears shimmered in the girl's eyes. Her rigid posture and fisted hands, said she wanted to be anywhere but there.

Rachel's heart twisted. She was one scared kid.

"Hi, Kayla. I'm Ms. Clark. Come on in." She walked over and met her at the door. "Your uncle and I were just talking about drama camp. We have some great things planned this summer." She tipped her head and smiled at Kayla. "How about you and I go get a soda in the lounge, and we can talk about it?"

Kayla pushed her hair over her shoulder with a trembling hand. "I'm not very good at drama."

"That's okay. A lot of the kids who come to camp have never been on stage before."

"I'll probably be the youngest one there and feel totally stupid."

"Actually, you're right in the middle age-wise. We have three groups—kids who are ten to twelve, thirteen to fourteen and fifteen to eighteen. Since you're turning fifteen pretty soon, you could try either of the older groups and see which one you like the best."

Her tense posture eased a bit. "Could I just watch the first day?"

"Sure. But I don't think you'll want to sit on the sidelines too long. Most of the activities are really fun, more like games."

"That sounds a whole lot more interesting than hanging out with me in the frame shop all day," Cam added.

Rachel laid her hand on Kayla's shoulder. "Come on. Let me show you around, and we can stop and get that drink I was talking about."

"I guess that would be okay." Kayla walked with her toward the door.

Rachel looked over her shoulder at Cam. "We'll check back with you later."

He mouthed the words, thank you, and sent her a heartfelt smile.

She suppressed a triumphant grin and looked back at Kayla. "The key to fitting in at drama camp is just being yourself. Everyone is a little nervous at first. That's totally normal. I'm sure in a couple days, you'll feel like you've been part of the group for a long time."

Chapter Eleven

Cam glanced at his watch and knocked on Kayla's bedroom door. She had retreated to her room as soon as they'd finished dinner about half an hour earlier, leaving all the dishes and clean up for him—again. He didn't mind the solo K.P. He was used to that. What he did mind was her ungrateful, sour attitude. For the past four days he'd tried to be patient and give her time to adjust, but all he got for his effort was an icy cold shoulder. "Kayla?" He knocked again, harder this time.

"What?" Even through the door he could hear her irritation loud and clear.

He swallowed his sharp reply. "May I come in?"

A couple seconds passed before she gave him permission.

He pushed opened the door, scanned the room and stopped cold. Clothes littered the floor. Dirty dishes,

DVD cases, soda cans and wadded up candy wrappers covered the top of the dresser and trunk. Kayla sat in the middle of it all, looking like the queen of clutter, enthroned on her bed with her computer open on her lap and her earphones plugged in.

His gut twisted. So much for the beautiful room he and Rachel had worked so hard to set up for her. "I'm going out back to water the garden."

She focused on her computer screen, ignoring him.

He clenched his jaw. "Take your earphones off," he growled.

She glared at him and slowly pulled them out.

"I'm going outside and I didn't want you to look for me and wonder where I was."

She lifted her brows, looking at him like that was the stupidest remark he'd ever made.

"Okay. That's it." He pointed his finger in her direction. "When I come back I want this room cleaned up."

She stared at him like he was speaking a foreign language.

"Did you hear what I said?"

She rolled her eyes. "I'm not deaf."

"Kayla—" he pulled in a deep breath and released it slowly "—I know you're not happy here. Believe me, I get it. But pouting and trashing your room isn't going to change anything."

She narrowed her eyes to a hateful glare. "You don't have a clue."

"Maybe not. But next time I see this room, it better be clean, or there will be consequences."

Her blue eyes flashed. "Like what?"

"Clean it up to my standards, or you'll have to say goodbye to your computer, iPod and phone."

She gasped. "You wouldn't!"

"Oh yes, I would. So you better get busy."

She slammed her computer closed and swung her legs over the side of the bed.

"The vacuum is in the hall closet. The cleaning supplies are under the kitchen sink." He pointed at the stack of dirty dishes on the dresser. "And be sure you load those into the dishwasher. I already cleaned the kitchen."

Her face flushed pink, and lips scrunched into a jagged line.

He checked his watch. "It's now seven fifteen. I'll give you until eight o'clock to get the job done."

Her mouth gaped open. "That's only forty-five minutes!"

"That's right, so you better get hoppin'."

She jumped to her feet. "Oooh! You are so… mean!"

He clamped his mouth shut and walked out the door. Heat pulsed from his face. His heart pounded like he'd just run a 5K race. That little girl had him totally tied up in knots. Closing his eyes, he tried to

calm his rushing thoughts. *Please, get her moving.
If I have to follow through, she is going to hate me
for the rest of her life.*

He opened his eyes, surprised he'd sent off a
prayer. He and the Almighty weren't exactly on
speaking terms—and for very good reasons.

Though he tried to stop them, memories swept
over him like a rising flood. Once again, he walked
the sterile hospital hallways, begging God to save his
wife. It was too late for his son. Tyler had died immediately. But after two agonizing days and countless
pleas, he had lost his wife as well.

If God wouldn't stoop down and save the life of a
faithful, loving woman like Marie, how could Cam
ever trust Him?

Rachel pulled the last plate from the rinse water
and set it on the counter to dry. Looking out her
kitchen window, she soaked in the peaceful view,
the gentle sway of the deep green fir trees lining
the backyard, the wide expanse of blue sky above.
A soft breeze floated through the screen, carrying
the sweet scent of roses from the trellis by the back
porch.

What a gift. She loved her apartment, the well-
kept yard and garden, the quiet neighborhood, and
the reassuring thought that Cam was right downstairs. For the first time in months she felt settled
and safe. No one would bother her here.

But memories of the troubled student who'd stalked her for months rose and taunted her, sending shivers up her arms. She swallowed and closed her eyes, wishing she could forget the terrible accusations he'd made against her. But that was impossible. The administration had called her in, the school board got involved, and the police grilled her with humiliating questions.

Of course she denied everything. She'd never had a romantic relationship with Kyle, but she was suspended from teaching while they conducted the investigation. Weeks of waiting and wondering what would happen just about sent her over the edge emotionally.

A lawyer from the teachers' union prevented the case from going to court, but by then two damaging articles had been printed in the *Seattle Times* for the whole world to read. When the charges against her were finally dropped, the *Times* gave the story one paragraph at the bottom of the obituary page.

But it was too late to save her reputation or her job. Kyle's lies convinced almost everyone she was the predator, and he was the victim. In the end her only option was resignation.

But that didn't satisfy Kyle. He'd continued to follow her and make her life a nightmare until she finally had to flee Seattle.

It was shocking that one unstable young man could unleash such a huge tidal wave of trouble simply because she refused his advances. But that was exactly what had happened.

She blew out a deep breath and tried to refocus her thoughts. *Father, please help me forgive Kyle and everyone who hurt me in Seattle. I know I've asked this so many times before, but I'm still struggling with it, and I need Your help. I believe You can somehow use all of this for good even though I can't see how right now. Help me hold on to that and trust You. Thank You for loving me and watching over me always.*

She stood still, with her eyes closed, waiting for peace to fill her heart. But instead, more troubling questions rose in her mind.

What if someone found out why she'd left her job in Seattle? She'd told Suzanne the basic facts when she applied for the job as director of N.C.Y.T., but she hadn't shared the whole story. She was afraid to be totally honest. Everything pointed toward her guilt. Hardly anyone in Seattle believed her, why would people in Fairhaven think any differently?

Bile rose and burned her throat. How could she build a new life on a shaky foundation of incriminating secrets? But she had no choice. The whole episode was humiliating, and she wasn't about to expose herself to that kind of scrutiny and condemnation again.

With a stubborn shake of her head, she wiped her hands on the dishtowel. Everything would be okay.

God would take care of her. Hadn't He proven that by bringing her to Fairhaven, giving her a new job, new friends and a chance to make a fresh start?

She was about to turn away from the window when Cam walked across the backyard. He tugged the hose along with him, his black T-shirt stretched tight across his broad chest and strong arms. But weary lines creased his forehead. Had he heard bad news from his sister? Whatever the problem, he looked like he needed a friend. She tucked her keys and cell phone into her pocket, and headed downstairs.

Cam waved to her as she crossed the brick patio. She slipped off her flip-flops and padded through the soft grass. Taking a seat on the stone bench under the cherry tree, she watched him set up the sprinkler. When he finished adjusting the water level, he walked over to her.

She smiled up at him. "Isn't it a beautiful evening?"

He scanned the sky frowning slightly. "Yeah. I guess it is."

She invited him to join her and slid down the bench to make room. He sat down and left a bit of space between them.

She waited while crickets chirped and insects buzzed. Finally she asked, "Everything okay?"

He sighed and crossed his arms. "Kayla is definitely not happy here. I'm worried about her."

She sent him a sympathetic smile. "It's not easy stepping into the parenting role."

"You're right about that."

"If it's any consolation, she seems to be doing better at camp. She chose to stay with the older group, and she's fitting in well."

"Yeah. Camp's the only thing she likes right now. Most mornings she's up and ready to go before I finish breakfast. Probably can't wait to get away from me."

Rachel grinned and bumped his shoulder with hers. "Ahh, don't take it personally. I'm sure she still loves you."

He shook his head. "Her last words to me were, 'you are so mean!'"

Rachel chuckled. "What did you do?"

"I told her she had to clean her room."

"It couldn't be that bad. She's only been here a few days."

"Oh, believe me, it's a disaster. Looks like a hurricane blew through."

Rachel covered her mouth to stifle her laughter.

"Go ahead and laugh, but when the health department condemns the house, you'll be out on the street, too!"

"So how did you convince her to see things your way?"

"I threatened to take away every piece of electronics she owns."

"Wow, you really know how to hurt a girl."

"Just trying to motivate her." His playful expression grew more serious. "I'm not sure what I'll do if she doesn't listen."

"Oh don't worry. She'll come around. No teenager wants to lose their connection to their friends."

"Hope so."

Rachel paused for few seconds. "Cleaning her room is important, but what about the other issues she's wrestling with?"

"She doesn't talk to me about anything."

"Maybe if you did something fun together, that might build a connection and help her feel more comfortable with you."

"Like what?"

"Well, what does she like to do?"

"I don't know. All I've seen her do is talk on the phone or watch movies on her computer."

"Then that's your first assignment. Find out what she likes to do for fun, and then make a date with her."

He frowned and rubbed his jaw. "But I'm a fly-fishing, ocean-kayaking, mountain-climbing kind of guy. What if she wants to go rollerblading or sight-seeing?" His face twisted into a painful grimace. "Or clothes shopping?"

"All the better." She turned and faced him. "If she sees you're willing to do something she loves, then it'll mean even more."

His gaze drifted toward the garden. "But how am I supposed to get past that mile-high wall she's put up."

"That's your challenge—get to know her so well you can scale that wall and win her heart."

He huffed. "I'm definitely not good at that."

She tipped her head and smiled. "Oh, I don't know."

He shifted and focused on her, unspoken questions in his blue eyes.

Her face flamed, and she looked away. Was she flirting with him?

"Thanks for the advice. Can't believe I'm so incompetent as a stand-in parent."

"This would be a challenge for anyone."

"It shouldn't be that hard for me." A shadow seemed to drop over his face. "My son, Tyler, would be seven this year."

Her heart clenched, and she swallowed. "I'm sure you were a wonderful father,"

"I wish that were true." He squinted toward the sinking sun.

She didn't know what else to say, so she laid her hand over his.

He blew out a soft breath. "I need to head back inside. I told Kayla I'd check her room." But rather than getting up, he turned his hand over and clasped hers. "Pray for me."

Her breath caught in her throat. "I will."

"Thanks." With a warm smile that tugged her heart toward his, he stood and walked back inside.

Why did his eyes seem to reflect so much guilt when he talked about his son's death? Facing the loss of a child had to be devastating for any parent, but both he and Hannah said a drunk driver caused the accident. It wasn't Cam's fault. Surely he didn't blame himself for his son's death, did he?

Chapter Twelve

"So, are you excited about the audition?" The light turned red as Cam's SUV rolled to a stop at the corner of Twelfth and Old Fairhaven Parkway.

"I guess." Kayla bit her lip and picked at the pink polish on her thumbnail.

"Do you have the sheet music for your song?" He should have asked her before they left home, but he still had time to go back if they needed to.

She glanced down at her backpack. "Yeah, I've got it."

He tapped on the steering wheel and shifted in his seat. Why was he so nervous? Kayla was the one trying out for a part in the summer musical.

The last forty-eight hours had been a crazy whirlwind. Everyone had to come to the audition prepared to sing a song from a musical. So he and Kayla had spent most of Friday afternoon searching through stores for the right sheet music. When they came up empty-handed, and Kayla was close to tears, Cam called Rachel. She helped Kayla calm down and put them in touch with Jack Herman, the N.C.Y.T. music director. He assured them he had the song she wanted to sing.

Kayla insisted she needed to have the music to practice, so they drove across town to pick it up, then stopped at a fast-food restaurant for dinner before returning home. So much drama over a three-minute song! But he didn't really mind. He was proud of her for having the courage to get up on stage and try out. Hopefully, she wouldn't bomb out and send her emotions on another rollercoaster ride.

He glanced across at Kayla. "I was thinking I'd come and watch you."

She turned and looked at him through wide eyes. "Why would you do that?"

He gave a half shrug. "I thought you might like someone in your corner to cheer you on." The light turned green and he drove through the intersection. "Rachel said most parents stay and watch."

She licked her lips and frowned out the front window. "Okay. But don't clap, and don't whistle, and don't do anything weird to embarrass me in front of my friends."

He stifled a groan and nodded. So much for scaling the wall and winning her heart.

Thirty minutes later he slipped into the auditorium balcony and quietly took a seat in the back row.

Hopefully, Kayla wouldn't notice him up there. If she made it through this first round with her song, then she'd have to read a monologue cold and finally take part in a group dance routine with just a few minutes of instruction. He intended to stay until the end. His stomach clenched at that thought. How would he soothe her crushed spirit if she failed to get a part?

Their disappointing conversation on the drive to the Arts Center replayed through his mind, and he sighed. He had hoped helping her prepare for the audition would draw them closer, but so far he hadn't seen much change in her attitude. Of course it had only been three days since Rachel encouraged him to look for ways to connect with Kayla and strengthen their relationship. It would probably take more time for his niece to see he was making an honest effort.

He scanned the kids seated in the center section of the auditorium, waiting for their turn to audition. Kayla sat in the third row, second from the end, between a short redheaded girl and a tall teenage boy with dark hair. The boy turned to Kayla and whispered something in her ear. She nodded and looked up at him with a dazzling smile.

Cam leaned forward, scowling. As he studied the boy's profile, recognition flashed through him. He was one of the kids who'd helped Rachel move into her apartment. Randy or Ryan. Yes, that was it. Well, *Ryan* had better behave himself around Kayla or he'd have to deal with Cam. He didn't intend to let anyone break her heart while she was in his care.

Cam huffed and sat back. Why was he so worried? Ryan was probably seventeen or eighteen since he was already driving and carrying passengers. A boy that age wouldn't be interested in dating a fourteen-year-old girl, would he?

Cam watched them carefully for a few more minutes, but didn't see anything out of line. He'd let it go for now, but he planned to keep an eye on that boy.

His gaze shifted to Rachel. She sat in the center of the first row with her head bent over her clipboard, jotting down notes. She leaned to the right and consulted Chandra about something, then Rachel stood and turned to the students. Her face glowed as she smiled at them. She obviously loved working with these kids, and from what he'd seen over the last few weeks, the kids loved her as well. They had a tight bond he admired, though sometimes it made him feel outside their circle.

"Okay, we're ready for the next age group, fourteen- to eighteen-year-olds." Rachel glanced at her clipboard. "Number fifteen, you're up."

The young girl at the end of Kayla's row left her seat and slowly climbed the stairs to the stage, her eyes wide and her hands clenched at her side.

Cam shook his head. The poor girl looked like she was terrified.

The girl made an awkward curtsy toward Rachel

and Chandra. "My name is Alyssa Morton. I'm four-teen years old, and I'll be singing 'Tomorrow' from *Annie*." She looked to the right where Jack Herman sat at the piano.

The music began, and the girl belted out the lyrics with more enthusiasm than talent. Cam winced and settled back in his chair.

The song ended, and the girl waited while her friends clapped. He was surprised at their encour-aging response. No one had laughed or whispered during her song. He supposed they all knew their turn would come to stand alone on stage, and that motivated them to support each other. Rachel had also probably taught them to show respect for each other during tryouts.

"Thanks, Alyssa." Rachel sent her an encouraging smile and gave her time to leave the stage before she called the next person. "Okay, number sixteen, your turn."

Kayla sprang from her seat, jogged up the steps, and crossed to center stage, her blond curls bouncing over her shoulders.

Cam gripped the armrests. She looked great, full of energy. The bright blue shirt she wore made her eyes stand out even from this distance. He closed his eyes for a brief second. *Please help her do well*.

Kayla faced Rachel and Chandra with a confident smile. "My name is Kayla Norton. I'm almost fifteen years old and I'd like to sing 'Somewhere over the

Rainbow' from the *Wizard of Oz*." She bowed her head and waited for the music to start.

The first few notes of the introduction flowed from the piano. Kayla took a deep breath and lifted her head. Her voice rose strong and clear, floating out over the auditorium like a sweet lullaby.

Cam's eyes widened, and the hair stood up on the back of his neck. She was good, very good. He'd heard her sing with Shannon and Eric at Christmas or goof around in the car when she sang along with the radio, but he had no idea she had so much power and range in her voice. A silly smile flooded his face.

Lifting her hand gracefully, she sang the next line, holding each note just the right length of time. Rachel nodded silently in time to the music, a smile on her lips and her total focus on Kayla.

When the song ended Kayla's fellow students burst into applause. The boy who had been seated next to her raised his fingers to his lips and let go an ear-splitting whistle. Kayla nodded her thanks, wearing a bright smile and flushed cheeks. Cam clapped loud and hard along with everyone else.

"Thank you, Kayla." Rachel turned and whispered something to Chandra, then jotted a note on her clipboard.

Kayla hurried down the steps and slipped back into her seat. Ryan gave her a pat on the back, and they exchanged a few words. Smiles wreathed both their faces.

Cam's mind spun as he watched them. Kayla wouldn't have any trouble capturing a role in the musical, but that might open the door to a whole new set of concerns when she started spending hours at rehearsals with Ryan and the other boys in the group. Though she was almost fifteen, she had lived a pretty sheltered life in Seattle as a homeschooler. It would be up to him to watch out for her and keep her safe. And that's exactly what he intended to do.

Rachel tiptoed up the steps and peeked through Cam's kitchen window. He stood at the sink, up to his elbows in suds, scrubbing away on a frying pan. She smiled as she watched him, and her stomach fluttered. Their lives seemed to intersect more every day, and she found it hard to ignore her growing feelings for him. She pulled in a deep breath and pushed that thought aside. Tonight was about Kayla. Maybe if she kept telling herself that she could stay focused and keep her feelings under control.

She tapped softly on the window. He looked up, and a smile spread across his face. She lifted her finger in front of her mouth, then pointed to the back door. The porch light flashed on as she crossed to meet him.

He pulled open the door, looking handsome in his faded jeans and light green polo shirt. "Hey."

She motioned him to come outside. "I need to talk to you, but I don't want Kayla to hear."

"She's in her room." He slipped out and quietly pulled the door shut behind him. "What's going on?" He moved closer, and the woodsy scent of his aftershave tickled her nose.

A shiver raced up her arms. She swallowed and pulled her thoughts back to the reason for her visit. "Kayla did a great job at the audition."

He grinned, and faint lines fanned out around his blue eyes. "Yeah. She was pretty amazing, wasn't she?"

"I didn't see you there."

"I was up in the balcony, under threat of death if I made a sound."

Rachel grinned. "She did well with her lines and the dance routine, and her voice is terrific."

Cam nodded and looked at her expectantly.

"So…I'm thinking of offering her the part of Anne, but I wanted to talk to you first."

He blew out a deep breath. "Wow. I'm sure she'd love to play the lead, but …" Concern shadowed his eyes. "I'm not sure she could handle that right now with everything else that's going on in her life."

Rachel nodded. "That's why I wanted to talk to you first. It would be a big commitment. She'd have a lot of lines and songs to learn, and she'd need to be at all the rehearsals. Everything builds toward our performances in late August." Rachel bit her lip. "Is she going to be in Fairhaven that long?"

"Yeah, she might even stay longer." He rubbed his forehead. "I know she really wants to be in the show, but is there any other part you could give her?"

"She could play Diana, Anne's best friend. It's a supporting role with fewer lines and less pressure."

He slipped his hands in his pockets. "That would probably be better for her."

She nodded, feeling as though a weight had been lifted from her shoulders. This was the right decision. She felt certain of it. "Her hair color might be a problem, but she could dye it."

Cam's eyes widened. "Dye those blond curls? No way! Shannon would kill me."

Rachel laughed. "The dye washes out, but I don't want to cause a family feud. We'll get her a wig."

"That would work." He shifted and concern filled his eyes. "Hey, I don't want to make a problem for you. Do you have someone else who can play Anne?"

Warmth wrapped around her heart. That was so sweet of him to think about her. "I'll give the part to Haley Mitchell. She's almost eighteen, so I thought she was too old to play Anne, but with the right makeup and costume she'll do fine."

He nodded, and his gaze drifted away. He shuffled across the porch and sat down on the top step.

Rachel sat next to him. "What is it, Cam?"

"I had a call from Shannon tonight."

"How's she doing?"

"She got some test results back today. The tumor is growing." His voice sounded strained, almost hoarse.

"Oh, Cam, I'm sorry."

"They're going to change the treatment plan, try something different. That's why I'm sure Kayla will be here at least through the end of August."

"How is she taking it?"

"I haven't told her yet. I don't want to scare her."

"Maybe it would be better if it came from Eric or Shannon."

"They were both pretty emotional last time we talked. They'll call again tomorrow around dinner-time. I have to tell her by then." He lowered his head.

Rachel's heart twisted, and she wished she could carry some of this burden for him.

"This whole thing is so unreal," he said. "That day I heard she had cancer again it felt as if I fell off a cliff and I haven't hit bottom yet."

She leaned closer until her shoulder touched his, hoping her nearness would comfort him.

"Why is this so hard?" he whispered.

Rachel's throat tightened, and she had to force out the words. "She's your sister, and you love her, that's why."

"Yeah, but it's got to be ten times worse for Kayla,

and I don't seem to have what it takes to help her through this."

"You're doing the best you can in a very difficult situation." They leaned against each other, warmth and comfort flowing between them while a soft cloak of evening fell around them.

"When Marie and Tyler died, there was no warning, no time to prepare. It was like a terrible explosion blew up my world. But with Shannon, the whole thing is strung out over months and years. The pain just goes on and on and never goes away."

She closed her eyes, praying for the right words. "That's a heavy load, Cam, too heavy for anyone to carry alone." Her voice was soft, just above a whisper.

"Yeah, you're right about that."

She sensed it was time to share at a deeper level. "God is there for you, Cam. He loves you, He'll help you carry this load."

Cam blinked, and his Adam's apple bobbed in his throat, but he didn't answer.

"Would you like to come to church with me tomorrow? I think you'd find a lot of encouragement there."

He huffed out a humorless chuckle. "I haven't been to church in years. The roof would probably cave in, if I walked through the door."

"Not at my church. We have lots of visitors every week. No one would make you feel uncomfortable."

He frowned and rubbed his chin. "I don't know."

"Shannon and Eric probably take Kayla to church every week. It would be good for her to have that kind of support."

He rolled his eyes. "Lay on the guilt, why don't you."

"Just stating the facts." She shrugged and grinned. "So, will you come with me tomorrow? I'll even let you sleep in and go to second service at eleven if you want."

He shifted away, breaking their connection.

Her hopes deflated, but she wasn't going to give up that easily. "Didn't you say you know my pastor, Sheldon James?"

He swatted at a moth circling around his head. "Yeah, Marie and I used to attend New Life Church in South Bellingham when he was pastor there."

She turned toward him. "Really?"

"Yeah, I know, shocking, right?"

She pulled in a sharp breath. "No, I didn't mean...I just didn't know you were involved in a church."

"Like I said, it's been a long time."

Her mind spun as she tried to sort out this new information. How long? Why had he stopped going? Had he made a sincere commitment, or was he just attending to please his wife?

The back door squeaked open. Kayla looked out through the screen. "Hey, I didn't know you guys were out here."

Cam scooted away and looked over his shoulder. "Come on out. We've got some good news for you." Then he shot a quick glance at Rachel with a hint of apology in his eyes.

Rachel smiled and sent him a slight nod. Maybe this news would cushion the blow Kayla would receive later when she heard about her mom's test results. "I was just talking to your uncle and getting his okay to offer you a part in the musical."

Kayla gasped, then ran over and knelt beside them. "Really? I got a part?"

Rachel nodded. "How would you like to play Diana?"

Kayla squealed and hugged Rachel. "I'd love it. Oh, I can't believe this." She turned and gave Cam a quick hug. "Thanks, Uncle Cam."

"What for?"

She shoved his shoulder playfully. "For running me all over town to get the music, and for cheering from the balcony."

His brows rose. "You saw me up there?"

"Of course I saw you. A big guy like you can't hide too easily."

Grinning, he tweaked her nose. "You are something else."

She gave him another little shove then turned

to Rachel, her eyes glowing. "Who's going to play Anne?"

"Sorry. I can't say. And you have to promise not to tell anyone about your part until the cast list is posted online tomorrow morning at nine."

Kayla gave them a solemn nod. "I promise, but it's going to be so hard." Her face lit up. "Could I please just tell my friend, Mandy, back in Seattle?"

Rachel tried to look stern, but she couldn't hold back a smile. "All right, but make her promise not to say anything to anyone until tomorrow morning."

"Okay. Thanks!" She dashed back in the house, the screen door slamming behind her.

Cam grinned as he watched her go. "You just made her one very happy girl."

Rachel returned his grin. "I'd say you played a big part in that, too."

Chapter Thirteen

Cam slid into the softly padded pew and glanced around the sanctuary of Grace Community Church. He didn't see anyone he recognized except Josh Crocker and his very pregnant wife, Suzanne, sitting in the row in front of them. He lowered his gaze to the bulletin in his hand and pulled in a deep breath.

When he'd walked in the front door of the church with Rachel and Kayla, Josh was the first one to greet him with a slap on the back and a firm handshake. Cam had turned several shades of red, remembering how he had treated Josh the day they helped Rachel move into her apartment.

Josh didn't seem bothered by any bad memories. In fact, the guy appeared downright happy to see him. He introduced Cam to his wife and even invited him to come out and watch the church softball team play Tuesday night. Cam couldn't get over that warm welcome. Did Josh treat every visitor like that?

Kayla leaned forward so she could see Rachel. "Do you think Ryan or any of the other kids from drama camp will be here?" Her eager expression put Cam on alert. No wonder Kayla had been so excited about coming to church when he'd mentioned it last night.

"They usually go to the early service," Rachel said. "But I'll let you know if I see them."

"Okay. Thanks." Kayla sat back, fiddling with her purse handle and watching people walk down the aisle.

Cam scanned the sanctuary, but he didn't see Pastor Sheldon James. He rubbed his sweaty hands on his pant legs. He hadn't spoken to Sheldon since Marie and Tyler's funeral more than four years ago. But that wasn't Sheldon's fault. Cam was the one who had ignored countless phone messages and e-mails from the man he had once considered his mentor and friend. Of course he'd see him today when he delivered the sermon, but what would he say if he ran into him afterward? His stomach tightened, and he lowered his head. Why had he agreed to come today?

Rachel touched his arm. "Everything okay?"

He straightened and looked into her big brown eyes, and he knew why he was here. When she'd invited him to church last night and looked at him with that same sweet concern, there was no way he could refuse. "Sure. Everything's fine."

She tilted her head toward him, and a whiff of a flowery fragrance floated his way. He pulled in a slow deep breath, and his tense shoulders relaxed. He could get used to being close to her like this.

"Did you have a chance to talk to Kayla about Shannon's test results?"

The question jerked him back to reality. "Not yet." He wanted his niece to enjoy the thrill of winning a role in the musical for a few more hours before he had to deliver the next round of bad news.

He looked up as seven members of the musical team walked onto the platform. Lyrics flashed on the large screen overhead. The buff bald man in the center invited everyone to stand, and the musicians began to play an upbeat song.

Cam wasn't familiar with it, so he listened as others around him sang. Kayla and Rachel's voices rose on either side. He finally joined in on the chorus. After a few more songs, it was time for announcements while ushers passed offering plates. Cam rummaged through his pocket and put in a ten-dollar bill as the plate came down the aisle.

Sheldon rose from his seat in the front row and walked up the steps to the podium. His confident gaze traveled over the congregation. Cam's breath hitched in his throat. Would Sheldon see him? No. There were at least four hundred people packed in this place. No way would Sheldon pick him out of this crowd. He released a deep breath and relaxed.

"Today we'll continue our study of the parables of Jesus. Please turn with me to Luke, chapter fifteen. We'll begin reading at verse eleven."

Rachel opened her Bible and quickly found the passage. She scooted a little closer to Cam, holding out her Bible so he could read along. Her arm touched his, and warmth radiated through him. He groaned under his breath, and told himself to focus on the verses, but sitting so close to Rachel made it a challenge.

"There was a man who had two sons. The younger one said to his father, 'Father, give me my share of the estate.' So he divided his property between them. Not long after that the younger son got together all he had and set off for a distant country, and there he squandered all his wealth on wild living."

Then Sheldon explained the story of the Prodigal Son in everyday language so no one would miss the meaning. "After the younger son's money was all gone, his so-called friends deserted him, and the only job he could find was working for a pig farmer. There he was, a good Jewish boy, slopping pigs. Not a very pretty picture. And he was so hungry he longed to eat the rotten food he poured in the pig's trough.

"He finally came to his senses and decided he would be better off at home. But he was ashamed of what he'd done, and he didn't feel worthy to be called a son, so he determined to confess it all to his father and ask for a job as a hired man."

Cam had heard the story many times before, but today it seemed to jump off the page and grab hold of his heart. Struck by the similarities to his life, he closed his eyes and gripped the edge of the pew.

Though he hadn't traveled to a distant land and lost all his money on wild living, he had wandered far away from his Heavenly Father, made some terrible mistakes and foolishly tried to hide how unworthy he felt to be called a son.

He thought avoiding his Christian friends and staying away from church would ease his guilt and bring him peace, but it hadn't. The distance he'd tried to keep between himself and God had only increased his pain and left him feeling broken and ashamed.

But how could he ever *go home* and face his Heavenly Father? He could never make up for what he had done to his wife and son.

He had insisted Marie drive that night. But the streets had been slick and icy. He should've seen the danger and protected his family, but he'd been too focused on himself—how tired he was from working all those long hours, how frustrated he was with his boss and coworkers, how disgusted he was with all the office politics—and his selfish choice had cost his wife and son their lives.

A black cloud of guilt descended over him. There

was no forgiveness for a crime like that. No way did he deserve to return to the Father.

Sheldon's voice broke through his thoughts. "But while he was still a long way off, his father saw him and was filled with compassion for him. He ran to his son, threw his arms around him and kissed him."

The story came to life in Cam's mind. He pictured the father embracing his son. Was that the way God felt about him? Would He really welcome him home with open arms if he simply confessed what he'd done and asked forgiveness? That seemed too simple. But that was how the father in the parable responded, pouring out his love and grace on the son even though he didn't deserve it.

His eyes burned. He lowered his head. *I'm sorry, God. So Sorry. If I could do it all over again, I'd take her place. I promise I would. Forgive me, God. Please forgive me.*

Rachel stilled as Cam bowed his head and closed his eyes, his struggle evident on his face.

Help him, Father. Do Your work in his heart, like a gentle, loving surgeon. Cut out what needs to be removed, and bring Your comfort and healing touch.

Pastor Sheldon continued, "The son said to him, 'Father, I have sinned against heaven and against you. I am no longer worthy to be called your son.'

But the father said to his servants, 'Quick! Bring the best robe and put it on him. Put a ring on his finger and sandals on his feet. Bring the fattened calf and kill it. Let's have a feast and celebrate. For this son of mine was dead and is alive again, he was lost and is found.'"

Cam lifted his head and gazed steadily at Sheldon.

Rachel's heart swelled. Surely, that was a message of hope that would comfort Cam, no matter what issues he wrestled with.

Maybe if she invited him to lunch after church he would talk to her about it. But Kayla would be there, and that would probably keep their conversation on a surface level.

Rachel released a soft sigh. She needed to relax and let God work on Cam's heart. Manipulating the situation or pressuring him to talk wasn't a good idea. No one liked to feel cornered about personal issues, especially spiritual ones.

But would he ever feel comfortable enough to share some of those deeper issues with her? She hoped so, because that level of sharing was important to her—and it was the only way she would know if she could truly trust him with her heart.

The rest of the service seemed to pass in a blur for Cam. As he bowed his head for the final prayer, he continued thinking about Sheldon's message. After a song and benediction, he stood and followed the crowd into the lobby.

"Oh, look. There's Ryan." Kayla waved to her friend. He stood on the far side of the lobby with three other guys who looked like college students. Ryan smiled her way. "Can I go talk to him for a few minutes?"

Cam glanced around for Rachel. Where was she? He needed backup.

Kayla tugged impatiently on his arm. "He's gonna leave if I don't hurry."

Cam frowned. "Isn't he a little old for you?"

Kayla rolled her eyes. "I'm not asking to go out with him. I just want to say hi."

Cam sighed. "All right. I'll wait for you by the refreshment table."

Rachel caught up with him and pulled a book from her purse. "I need to give this to my friend, Katy. It'll just take me a minute to zip down to the nursery." She hesitated. "Do you want to come, or wait here?"

He didn't want her to think he couldn't handle a few minutes alone in the church lobby. "Go ahead. I'll grab a cup of coffee."

She sent him a bright smile. "Okay. Be right back." She disappeared into the crowd.

The aroma of fresh-brewed coffee drew Cam across the lobby. Three tall steaming coffee makers were set up on a table along with trays of donuts and bagels. He filled a cup and dumped in plenty of cream and sugar, then took his time stirring. Hopefully, he wouldn't have to speak to anyone while he waited for Rachel and Kayla. He took a sip and turned around.

Sheldon stood about ten feet away talking to an elderly woman in a faded-green raincoat. He bent toward her and took her hand, as though he wanted to catch every word she said.

Cam's stomach churned. Should he walk away or stay and face Sheldon?

Before he could decide, something broke Sheldon's concentration, and he looked Cam's way. Recognition flashed in his warm brown eyes, and he straightened.

Cam froze. Heat burned up his neck and into his face.

Sheldon gave the elderly woman a gentle hug. Then, with a smile spreading wider, he headed toward Cam with open arms.

Cam set down his coffee and met him halfway. As they embraced, moisture filled Cam's eyes, and he quickly blinked it away.

"It's great to see you, Cam." Sheldon slapped Cam a couple times on the back. Then he stood back and looked him over, his smile radiating genuine warmth and welcome.

"Good to see you, too." Cam cleared his throat

and shifted his weight to the other foot. "That was a good message. It really hit home."

Sheldon's gaze met his. "Finding your way home is worth the journey, no matter how far you have to travel or how long it takes."

Cam swallowed against his tight throat. "Yeah, you're right about that."

Sheldon reached in his pocket and pulled out a business card. "Why don't you give me a call this week? I'd like to get together." The sincerity in his voice was unmistakable.

Cam took the card and glanced at the number. Part of him wanted to jam the card in his pocket and pretend he hadn't seen Sheldon, but the longing to restore their friendship won out, and he nodded. "Okay. I'll give you a call."

"Great. I'm glad you came today."

Cam tucked the card in his shirt pocket and nodded. "So am I."

Chapter Fourteen

Rachel pulled the picnic basket down from the top shelf in the hall closet and carried it into the kitchen. The sun's rays slanted through the kitchen window sending long amber shadows across the tile floor. A cricket serenade rose from the backyard, and a warm breeze floated through the open window.

She glanced at the clock. It was almost seven. She had better get moving if she was going to have some snacks packed and ready when Cam came knocking at her door.

She smiled, remembering the sneaky way Kayla had arranged the plans for this evening. That girl was turning into quite a little matchmaker. Or maybe her schemes had more to do with her own interest in a certain young man at N.C.Y.T. than any thoughts she might have about getting Cam and Rachel together. As she filled the basket, the scene from yesterday afternoon replayed in her mind.

Cam walked down the aisle of the Arts Center auditorium and met Rachel in front of the stage. "So, how did rehearsal go? Everyone excited to get started?"

"Too excited. I could hardly get them to settle down. I have to be pretty strict these first few rehearsals."

"I see." Cam nodded and sent her a warm smile. "Hope you let them have a little fun."

"A little." She studied his face. Something was different about him the last few days. He hadn't explained what was going on, but she suspected it had something to do with his visit to Grace Chapel last Sunday. Whatever the reason, he definitely seemed less brooding and more hopeful.

He cocked his head. "What? Why are you looking at me like that?"

Warmth flooded her face. "No reason." She turned and glanced at the students gathered on the stage.

Kayla broke away from the group pulling fifteen-year-old Lindsey Parker with her. The girls trotted down the steps, grinning and whispering as they approached. "Hey, Uncle Cam, what are we doing tomorrow night?"

"I'm not sure, why?"

"They're showing the movie *The King and I* on the Village Green, and we want to go. Could you give us a ride?"

"I don't think your parents would want you to go out at night by yourselves."

"Oh, we wouldn't be by ourselves," Lindsey added, her face all innocence. "A whole bunch of kids are going."

Cam narrowed his eyes. "Like who, Ryan and Steve?"

Kayla's face turned bright pink, and she shrugged. "Probably."

"Then I don't think so."

"Come on, Uncle Cam. It's a G-rated move." She bit her lip, her eyes pleading. "I guess you could come along, if you want to."

"Oh, that would be fun. You'd take off with your friends, and I'd end up sitting there all by myself." He shook his head. "No thanks."

Kayla's eyes widened. "I know. Why don't you bring a friend?" She grinned at Rachel and wiggled her eyebrows.

Rachel laughed to hide her embarrassment.

A mischievous glint lit Cam's eyes. "Well, I suppose I could ask Ross and see if he has plans."

Kayla scowled. "Not Ross! Ask Ms. Clark."

"Yeah, Come on, Mr. McKenna, ask her," Lindsey added with a delighted grin.

Cam tucked his hands in his jeans pockets and rocked back on his heels. "Would you like to go see the movie with us?"

"Hmm." She tapped her cheek, teasing him with

her smile. "I don't know. Ross might feel left out if you don't invite him."

"I don't think he likes musicals."

"Well, in that case, I suppose I could go."

"Yes!" Kayla grabbed Lindsey's arm. "Come on, let's go tell everyone we'll be there."

Cam leaned toward Rachel. "Now we're really in trouble."

"Why?"

"We've just made ourselves chaperones for the whole group. Can't you hear them all telling their parents, 'Oh, it's okay. Ms. Clark and Mr. McKenna are going to be there with us.'"

Her stomach clenched. Would her students wrangle permission from their parents by telling them she was overseeing the group? What if something happened to one of the kids while she was supposedly in charge? Memories of angry confrontations with parents in Seattle flooded back, sending a sickening wave of dread through her. She never wanted to go through something like that again.

He touched her arm. "Hey, I was just kidding. It's not an official field trip."

"Right." She tried to shake off her apprehension, but it followed her all afternoon.

Her doorbell rang, bringing her back to the moment. "Coming," she called, then took the basket and headed down the stairs.

Cam smiled at her through the screen door. "Ready to go?"

She nodded, and a calming wave washed over her, easing her fears. Nothing bad would happen tonight. And on the slight chance that there was a problem, Cam would be there to help. She wouldn't have to face a group of angry parents alone.

Twenty minutes later Rachel and Cam wove their way through the crowd on the Fairhaven Village Green followed by Kayla and Lindsey. Groups of people had spread blankets on the grass, while others sat in portable lawn chairs on the brick walkways under the pergola that ran around the sides of the Green. Up on stage, a three-person musical group sang folk songs as pre-movie entertainment.

"How about over there?" Cam pointed to an open spot across the way.

"That looks good." Rachel followed Cam past a young couple eating Chinese takeout, a giggling group of elementary-age girls playing rummy and an older couple keeping a little toddler entertained. They spread out their blanket, and Rachel sat down on one side. Cam settled in next to her while the girls stood nearby on the grass.

Lindsey leaned toward Kayla. "Do you see them?"

"Not yet." Kayla continued scanning the crowd, then gave a little squeal. "There they are." She grabbed Lindsey's arm. "Let's go."

Cam tugged on Kayla's pants leg. "Wait a minute. Where are you two headed?"

"We're just going over there to see our friends."

Cam frowned, looking as though he wanted to say no. Rachel touched his arm. They exchanged a glance, and he released his hold on Kayla's pants leg. "Okay. But be back before the movie starts."

The girls dashed away. Rachel leaned to the left and watched them make a beeline for Ryan and Steve, who stood under the pergola near the Colophon Café with Haley, Danielle and a couple other kids she didn't recognize.

Cam sighed. "I guess I need to lighten up, but I hate to see what will happen if one of her friends lets her down tonight. Her emotions have been on a wild ride this week."

"That sounds pretty normal for a girl her age."

"Maybe so, but I'm still not used to it."

Rachel took the bag of popcorn from the basket and offered some to Cam. "There is something I wanted to let you know."

"About Kayla?"

Rachel nodded. "She's been sitting with Ryan a lot at rehearsals. Some of the kids are starting to talk about it."

Cam frowned. "Do you think he likes her?"

"I'm not sure. He's a really friendly guy, so it's hard to tell if he's treating Kayla special or not."

Cam's frown deepened. "I sure don't want to see

her get her heart broken by some guy who doesn't even know she exists."

Rachel smiled. "Oh, he knows."

"Great. Is that good news or bad news?"

She leaned back, bracing her hands behind her on the blanket. "Ryan is a good kid. He goes to Grace Chapel with his family. But I'll keep an eye on him and Kayla and let you know if I see anything to be concerned about."

"Thanks. She's young and naive. I just don't want anyone to hurt her."

Rachel studied Cam, replaying his caring words. By the time she was Kayla's age, her father had long since disappeared. She'd never had an uncle or brother to step in and protect her. Was that why she'd gone from one hurtful relationship to the next in high school and college, always searching for the love she hadn't received from a special man in her life?

When she became a Christian in her mid-twenties, she pulled back from dating, confused by her past and uncertain how it fit in with her new faith.

"What are you thinking?" He leaned closer and traced his finger around her hand as though he was drawing the pattern on the blanket.

His nearness and touch stirred her heart. "I was just wondering how my life would've been different if I'd had someone like you watching out for me when I was Kayla's age."

He looked at her with a tender gaze. "I wish I would have known you then."

She smiled, but looked away as heat filled her face. "I don't know if you would've felt that way if you'd seen me back then. I had braces, and I was so skinny people called me beanpole."

He chuckled. "I was short and chubby with a wild blond *'fro.*" He pointed to his hair. "We would've been perfect together."

"You were chubby?" She laughed and poked his stomach. "I don't believe it."

He lifted two fingers. "Scout's honor. But when I turned sixteen, I went out for football and grew about five inches. That took care of everything but the hair."

"I love your hair." The words slipped out before she realized what she was saying.

He looked up, and his gaze connected with hers for several seconds. Electricity seemed to charge the air between them. "What service are you going to tomorrow?"

She blinked, and a smile broke over her face. "Whichever one you want."

He laughed softly. "How about we try early service?"

"Sounds good." A happy, light feeling filled her heart. Their friendship seemed to be turning a corner, but she still wanted to know what was going on in his heart. "So…what happened last Sunday?"

"What do you mean?"

"You seem different this week, more hopeful."

He sat up and looked out across the Village Green. "Sheldon's message really made me think."

"In what way?"

"I've heard that story of the Prodigal Son before. But this time I realized God is a lot like that father. He's waiting with open arms and willing to forgive if we'll just come home and admit the truth about the mess we've made of our lives."

She nodded slowly, her heart rejoicing. "So are you and God back on speaking terms?"

"We're working on it." He took another handful of popcorn and munched for a few seconds. "I got together with Sheldon this week."

She wanted to jump up and shout "yes!" But she forced herself to sit still. "How did that go?"

"It went well. He's a lot like that father in the Prodigal Son story." A slight smile lifted the corners of his mouth. "It'll take a while for us to rebuild our friendship, but we're both committed to that."

"Wow. That's great. I didn't realize you two... knew each other like that."

Cam looked down and brushed a piece of popcorn from his leg. "He performed our wedding."

She nodded, her heart touched again by the losses he'd experienced. "Sounds like you're on a good path, Cam. I'm happy for you."

"Thanks. It's taken me a while, but I think I'm

ready to move on to whatever God has for me in this next phase of life." His voice sounded strong and steady, and the look in his eyes told her he wasn't only thinking about getting closer to God. He was talking about a relationship with her.

Her heartbeat quickened. Was she ready to take the next step with Cam? Her past history with men and the poor choices she'd made sent doubts swirling through her mind. But Cam was different, wasn't he?

She pulled in a slow deep breath. There was no need to feel pressured or make any decisions tonight. She had time to pray and see what would develop. But she realized her heart had already made up its mind.

The music group ended their song and announced the movie would start in a few minutes.

Cam straightened and looked around. "Do you see Kayla?"

Rachel glanced across the Green, but she didn't see her. "Maybe they found a place to sit together." She searched the crowd, but the sun had set, making it harder to see anyone clearly.

A worried frown creased Cam's forehead as he got up. "I'm going to look for her."

Rachel stood. "I'll help."

"Okay." They agreed to split the Green and each cover one half. "If you find her, tell her she has to come back and sit with us. No excuses." His voice was stern, but she saw the anxiety in his eyes.

Rachel squeezed his hand. "Don't worry. I'm sure she's okay."

He nodded and headed off like a man on a mission.

Rachel searched the crowd as she made her way toward the pergola at the north end of the Green. Intro music for the movie played. She spotted Haley in line at the refreshment stand and asked her if she'd seen Kayla.

"She and Lindsey were with Steve and Ryan over by Village Books a few minutes ago. I think they were going in to buy coffee."

"Okay thanks." Hopefully, she'd still find them there. She spun around and bumped into Melanie Howard.

The drink in Melanie's hand sloshed down her shirt. She gasped and cursed under her breath.

Rachel pulled back. "Oh, I'm sorry. I didn't see you."

"Obviously!" Melanie glared at her as she shook the soda off her hands.

"Here, let me help." Rachel pulled a couple clean tissues from her pocket and held them out to Melanie. "Do you want me to go get some napkins or a towel or something?"

Melanie huffed. "You can drop the act."

"Excuse me?"

"You heard what I said. You can forget the nice-girl routine."

Rachel stared at Melanie. Of course she knew Melanie didn't like her. She'd made that clear often enough. "I meant what I said. I'm sorry about running into you." Rachel wanted to say more, but she swallowed the words and turned away.

"Hold on." Melanie stepped into her path. "You and I need to get a few things straight."

Rachel tensed, her anger simmering just below the surface. "Like what?"

"I know you're here with Cam."

"That's right. Is that a problem for you?"

Melanie's nostrils flared. "Yes. It is. I care about Cam. He's been through a lot over the last few years, and I've been there for him. We were getting really close until you showed up and wormed your way into his life."

Rachel's mouth dropped open.

"You're not fooling me." Melanie looked at her with a haughty glare. "I know what you're after."

"What are you talking about?"

"You think if you can convince Cam you care about him, then your drama program can stay at the Arts Center."

"I'm not trying to convince Cam of anything."

"Oh, right. It's been obvious since you put on that big act at the first co-op meeting, when you told us how your poor little kids would be out in the cold unless we rented you some space. And Cam's got such a big heart, he can't resist rescuing an underdog." She pushed her blond hair over her shoulder. "And that's exactly what he sees when he looks at you—a loser who needs to be rescued."

"You have no idea what you're talking about." She stepped away from Melanie.

But the blond clamped onto Rachel's arm. "I'm warning you. If you hurt Cam, you'll be sorry you ever came to the Arts Center."

Rachel jerked her arm away. "Are you threatening me?"

"I'm saying you need to back off."

"Rachel?" Cam's voice cut through the cool evening air.

She looked up, her heart pounding in her throat.

Cam crossed the grass and met them on the brick walkway. "I found Kayla and Lindsey."

She pulled in a quick breath and tried to steady her voice. "Are they okay?"

"Yeah. They're fine." He nodded to Melanie, and then frowned slightly at her stained shirt. "Looks like you spilled something."

Melanie gave an indignant sniff. "Rachel rammed into me like a linebacker."

Cam looked back and forth between them, then took Rachel's hand. "We better go. We're missing the movie." He sent the fuming blond one last look. "See you, Mel."

Triumph pulsed through Rachel. She leaned toward Cam as they walked away. "Thank you."

He cocked his head. "What for?"

"For rescuing me from the dragon."

He grinned. "Ah, don't worry about Melanie. She'll get over it."

"You think so?" She studied his face, trying to discern how much he'd heard.

"Sure. Soon as she washes that stain out of her shirt, she'll forget the whole thing ever happened."

Rachel released a shaky breath. He obviously hadn't heard Melanie's awful accusations. Maybe she should tell Cam what Melanie said, but then she'd have to admit there was an ounce of truth mixed in with the pound of misperceptions.

At first she had wanted to win Cam over and make sure N.C.Y.T. had a permanent home. But things were different now. She liked Cam, and she was beginning to think he felt the same way about her.

What would Melanie do when she realized her threats were not going to change Rachel's mind?

Chapter Fifteen

Cam strode into Ross's photography studio looking for his friend, but he didn't see him in the gallery area. Cam suspected he was still in the back taking photos of Kayla, but he didn't mind waiting.

He glanced at the pictures on display. Of course he'd seen them all before when Ross brought them in to be framed, but it was different viewing them grouped together on the wall.

Ross had an artist's eye. It was obvious why he won photography competitions all over the state.

He studied the photo of the old W.P.A. bridge near Whatcom Falls. The contrast of the sturdy old stone arches and lush green forest made it one of his favorites. That was a great spot. He'd have to take Rachel there some time soon. That idea brought a smile to his face.

Rachel was the first woman he'd been interested in since losing Marie. Even now, thinking about someone else like that felt a little strange. But he'd enjoyed their movie date on the Village Green. And each time they were together he found more things he appreciated about her, like her dedication to her students, her strong faith and her positive view of life. Their connection was definitely growing deeper.

Was he man enough to do things differently this time? He better be, because the thought of hurting Rachel the way he'd hurt Marie was too painful to consider. Surely with his renewed faith and a little help from Sheldon, he could build a solid relationship.

The sound of Ross's voice from down the hall made Cam shift gears.

"Okay, now turn to the left just a little. Great. Hold it right there." A series of camera clicks sounded. "Lift your chin and look this way. Awesome."

Cam walked down the hall to the second room. Kayla sat on a stool in front of a soft-blue backdrop. Bright lights flooded the area around her. She wore a brilliant smile, and her blue eyes sparkled as she posed for the camera.

"Your mom is going to love these." Ross clicked off another series of shots.

"When will I get to see them?" Kayla asked.

"Soon as we're done you can take a look and pick out your favorites."

Cam stepped up behind Ross. "How's it going?"

"Great. Look at that face. Kayla could be a model."

That comment made her smile brighten. "He's taken about a hundred pictures."

Cam grinned. It was good to see her so happy. This morning they'd both been in a panic when they realized Shannon's birthday was only five days away, and they had no idea what to send her. Cam sent off an emergency prayer, and within minutes, an idea came to mind. He'd whispered a prayer of thanks and called Ross. His friend was eager to help and promised to print the photos right away so they could get them in the mail by late afternoon. Hopefully, the birthday package would arrive on time and lift Shannon's spirits.

"Okay. I think we've got what we need." Ross connected his camera to the computer on his desk, and a few seconds later he invited Kayla over to take a look.

She hopped up from the stool and took a seat at Ross's desk. "You want to see them, Uncle Cam?"

"Why don't you do the first round, then I'll take a look after?"

"Okay." She turned and focused on the computer screen.

Cam slapped Ross on the back. "Thanks for doing this. I know it will mean a lot to Shannon and Eric."

"My pleasure." Ross motioned Cam out to the

hallway. They walked away from the open door. "How's your sister doing?"

Cam lowered his voice to make sure Kayla wouldn't overhear their conversation. "She got some more test results back yesterday. There's no change in the tumor." Saying the words aloud made his chest feel tight.

"Is that bad news?"

"They want the tumor to shrink."

Ross nodded, his expression serious. "How's Kayla doing?"

"She has her ups and downs, but she seems to be doing better since she connected with the kids through drama camp." Cam slipped his hands in his pockets. "She gave me a real run for my money those first couple weeks. If Rachel hadn't been around to give me some good advice, I'd have really blown it."

Ross grinned and pushed his glasses up his nose. "Hey, I hear you had a hot date with Rachel on Saturday night."

Cam frowned. "Who told you that?"

"Lilly. She said Melanie saw you two at the movies."

"The real story is I took Kayla and her friend to a movie, and I happened to invite Rachel to come along."

Ross wiggled his eyebrows and sent him a mischievous grin. "So…how did it go?"

"Great, until Kayla disappeared. Then Rachel and I had to split up and search for her. Rachel ran into Melanie and accidentally dumped a coke down her shirt. That ticked Melanie off, and I got there just in time to rescue Rachel."

Ross frowned and crossed his arms. "You need to have a talk with her."

"Who? Melanie?"

"Yes. She's been saying some pretty awful things about Rachel. I think she's just mad you're spending time with Rachel instead of her."

Cam huffed out a disgusted breath. "What is this, high school?"

Ross shrugged. "I just thought you'd want to know what she's up to."

"All Melanie wants is attention—my attention—and I'm not giving it to her." He jabbed his friend in the chest. "And don't you listen to her when she starts off on one of her diatribes."

Ross squinted at him. "Her what?"

"*Diatribes.* It means verbal attacks."

"Oh, right."

"Hey, I thought you graduated from college."

Ross pulled away. "You know I did."

"Then how come you don't know what *diatribe* means?"

Ross glared at him. "My major was photography, not crossword puzzles like yours."

Cam slapped his friend's shoulder. "Right. I

shouldn't be giving you a hard time. I got an MBA, and look at me—I'm a framer."

Ross's eyes widened. "You got an MBA? How come you never told me that?"

"I told you. You just weren't listening." He punched his friend's arm. "Now, promise you'll use that same skill and turn a deaf ear the next time Melanie starts to gossip about Rachel or anyone else."

"Okay, okay." He held up his hand to ward off another punch. "I'll tell her to put a cork in it the next time she spouts a bitter *diatribe*. But you've got to promise me one thing."

"What's that?"

"Stop using me for a punching bag."

"Sure. I was just playing around."

Ross winced and rubbed his arm. "Yeah. Right."

"Let's try it again from the top." Rachel nodded to Jack Herman. He focused on the sheet music and played the intro to the song "Kindred Spirits." Several of the student actors sat quietly in the first two rows. Chandra stood stage left with Kayla, and Haley waited at center stage, listening for the right time to come in.

Rachel smiled. *Thank You, Lord, for helping me choose the right person for each part.*

Kayla would've been a wonderful Anne, but Haley's experience and maturity had a positive impact on everyone. She continually encouraged her friends. And her comfortable friendship with Ryan, who played Gil, made their on-stage romance a bit easier to deal with.

Kayla's crush on Ryan had become more obvious over the last week, and Cam wasn't too happy about it. That was another reason she was thankful she had included Cam in the decision to cast Kayla as Diana rather than Anne.

Rachel tapped her foot in time to the music, watching the girls move through the new choreography Chandra had taught them that afternoon. Their movements were still stiff, but they would smooth out as they practiced together over the next month.

Rachel was so focused she didn't realize Cam had stepped up beside her until he placed his hand on her back.

Warmed by his touch, she looked up and smiled. "Hi."

He returned her smile. "How is it going?"

"Great. Chandra is working with them on a new song."

He shifted his gaze to Kayla. "She's doing okay?"

Rachel nodded. "She's amazing, especially for someone without a dance background."

His eyes glowed as he watched his niece glide across the stage. "Her parents are going to be so proud of her."

"Do you think they'll be back in time to see a performance?"

The light faded from his eyes. "I don't know."

She reached for his hand. "I'll be praying they make it home by then."

He tightened his fingers around hers. "Being in the show means a lot to her. It's given Kayla a positive focus so she doesn't worry about her mom as much."

"I'm glad."

He turned and looked into her eyes. "Thanks for what you're doing, not just for Kayla, but for all the kids. I can see how they're all learning a lot, and it gives each one an opportunity to shine. That's pretty special."

Her heart felt like a helium balloon rising in the sky. He got it! Knowing he understood why she poured out her heart to help the kids develop their talents and become the people God wanted them to be was such a special gift.

She smiled up at him. "That's the sweetest thing anyone has said to me in a long time." Then she stood on tiptoe and kissed his cheek. "Thank you."

He grinned. "Wow. Guess I'll have to think of some more brilliant things to say if I'm going to get a reaction like that."

Rachel laughed and gave him a playful nudge with her shoulder.

"Cam?" Hannah Bodine bustled down the aisle toward them.

Cam turned and greeted her.

"We have a problem." She motioned them to the side of the auditorium. "My nephew, Ron, is on the school board. And last night at the meeting they discussed overcrowding in the elementary school." Her brows twitched. "One of the board members suggested selling our building and using the funds to add a new wing to the existing school."

Rachel gasped. "Are they serious?"

"I'm afraid they are."

"But what about the money we pay them each month?" Rachel asked.

"That money only covers the expenses of maintaining the building."

Rachel gripped her clipboard. "So what did they decide?"

"Nothing yet. But they appointed a group to look into it and report back next month."

Cam nodded slowly and crossed his arms. "Okay. That gives us some time."

Rachel stared at him. How could he be so calm? "They can't make a decision like that without talking to us, can they? Don't they have to have a public meeting so we can discuss the idea?"

Cam laid his hand on her shoulder. "We don't know what they're going to do yet, or how much they'll involve us in the process."

Rachel tensed under his touch. Of course moving to a new location wouldn't be a problem for him. He could put a frame shop anywhere, but finding another home for N.C.Y.T. would be a huge challenge and disruption to their program.

"I think all the co-op partners need to know what's going on," Hannah added.

"I'll see if we can set up a meeting tonight." Cam turned to Rachel. "I don't think we need to worry. It's just an idea right now."

Rachel met his gaze. "If that idea becomes a reality, we're all going to lose something very important. I hope you're taking this seriously."

"Keeping the co-op together is top priority for me. We'll fight this if we have to, but I don't want to waste time worrying about something that may never happen."

Rachel pulled in a calming breath. Cam was right. It was time to be calm and logical, not let her fears run away with her good sense.

Chandra called her name from the stage. The music had stopped. It was time to end rehearsal and send the kids home.

"Okay, everyone," Rachel called. "Let's huddle up." She gathered the kids in a circle and asked Steve to pray.

He bowed his head, and the other kids followed. "Father, thanks for a good rehearsal. Help us all to learn our parts and do our best. Please watch over us, keep us safe and bring us back together again tomorrow. Amen."

Short and sweet. She smiled her approval and dismissed the kids.

If only all the problems of the world could be solved with a simple little prayer like that.

"I don't believe this!" Melanie's eyes flashed, and she slapped her hand down on Lilly's table. "How can they sell the building right out from under us? Doesn't our lease mean anything?"

Rachel glanced around the table at her co-op partners. Everyone was upset by the news Cam had shared, but Melanie's reaction was over the top.

"We don't know if our lease will protect us or not." Ross leaned forward. "That's why I think we need to contact a lawyer."

"How much will that cost?" Lilly asked, lines creasing her brow.

"I'm not sure, but I have a friend who might be willing to give us some free advice, or at least a discount."

"The museum can't afford to hire lawyer," Hannah added. "And we certainly don't have money to relocate."

Melanie's nostrils flared. "So, are we just going to sit back and let them run us out of here? Let's take the offensive and threaten those board members with a lawsuit. That will make them sit up and think twice about kicking us out."

Everyone's voices blended together as they responded to Melanie's idea.

Cam held up his hand. "All right. Let's settle down. First of all, No one is kicking us out yet. We don't know if the board will follow through on this or not. And even if they do decide to sell, who is going to buy a building like this?"

"Developers are buying properties all over Bellingham, especially in Fairhaven," Hannah added.

Lilly's face lit up. "Maybe we could rent from the new owner."

"What if they want to tear the building down or turn it into a strip mall?" Ross said.

There had to be something they could do. Rachel sat up straighter. "I know. Why don't we buy the building?"

Melanie huffed. "Oh right, like we all have stacks of money just sitting in our bank accounts."

"We might not have enough individually, but if we put our money and credit backing together, we might be able to buy it." Rachel didn't know much about business loans, and she certainly didn't have much she could contribute toward a down payment, but maybe the others did. She looked around the table.

Cam sent her an apologetic half smile. "Buying

the building would be great, but most of us invested our savings in renovations."

"Then let's raise the money," Rachel said.

"How would we do that?" Lilly asked.

"We could become a non-profit group and apply for grants from foundations that support the arts. Or maybe we could look for other ways to raise funds."

"Right, like bake sales and car washes," Melanie added with a sarcastic sneer. "We'd never get enough money together in one month."

Rachel turned away from Melanie. "We don't know how quickly the board will move on this. We could at least see what's involved and start the process."

Ross tapped his pencil on the table. "Or we could look for a new location." Lilly moaned and Hannah shook her head, then Ross continued. "I know none of us likes the idea of moving, but if we found a building in the historic district, it might put us closer to the other stores and galleries."

"We tried that," Lilly said. "But all those buildings were out of our price range, remember?"

Ross sighed. "Yeah, I remember."

Cam flipped his yellow pad to a new page. "Okay. It's getting late. Let's make a plan. Hannah, why don't you stay in touch with Ron and see what else he can find out for us. Rachel, would you look into what's involved in setting up a non-profit and going after some grant money?"

"Sure." Rachel nodded to Cam, then made a note for herself.

Melanie glared at Rachel, clearly perturbed.

"Ross, why don't you talk to your lawyer friend and see what it would cost for him to help us. I'll contact a real estate agent and see if there are any buildings nearby that would meet our needs. Lilly and Melanie, maybe you can ask around about any possible places that aren't listed with a Realtor yet."

Melanie lifted her eyes toward the ceiling. "How in the world am I supposed to find those? You want magic. Ask a magician."

Lilly ignored Melanie and nodded to Cam. "I'll talk to a few people and see what I can come up with."

"Okay. Thanks." Cam glanced around the table. "And it wouldn't hurt to say a prayer or two about this situation. We need all the help we can get."

"Amen to that!" Hannah added with a pleased grin.

Rachel nodded and sent him a warm smile.

Fifteen minutes later Rachel locked her office door and joined Cam in the hallway. She fell into step beside him as they headed toward the front door of the Arts Center. "You did a good job tonight. It's not easy to lead a meeting when everyone's emotions are running so high."

He held the door open so she could pass through first. "Melanie and Hannah still seem pretty upset even though we came up with some good ideas," Cam said.

Warm, sea-scented air greeted Rachel as she stepped outside. "Well, it's a scary situation for all of us."

"But it doesn't seem to be affecting you the same way it does the rest of them," Cam replied.

She tipped her head, remembering how anxious she'd been that afternoon when she'd first heard the news. "I don't like the prospect of searching for a new location any more than they do. But I took some time to pray before the meeting, and that helped.

"I'm always telling the kids, 'Don't worry. God's big enough to handle any problem that comes your way. He has a plan, and He's got everything under control.' If I believe that then I don't need to be afraid of whatever is coming."

He slipped his arm around her shoulder as they stepped off the curb. "That's one of the things I like about you. You let your faith impact how you think and what you do every day."

She smiled and ducked her head. "That's sweet, Cam."

"I mean it, Rachel. I don't know many people who

live what they believe the way you do. You make me want that kind of faith for myself."

His words made her feel like dancing. If watching her go through tough times stirred up that kind of response in Cam's heart, it was worth it all.

They stopped beside her car, and he waited while she searched through her purse and found her keys.

He laid his hand over hers. "Wait."

She stilled and looked up at him.

A tender message flowed from his eyes as he lifted his hand and traced his fingers down her cheek. "Rachel...you're a treasure." He lowered his head, moving closer.

She lifted her face and her eyes drifted closed. His kiss was slow and sweet and achingly tender, melting away all her questions and worries.

Finally, he stepped back. "Wow. That was great. Maybe we should try that again." Mischief twinkled in his eyes.

She laughed softly and squeezed his hand. "I better go." But she stood on tiptoe and kissed his cheek before she climbed into her car. "Good night, Cam. I'll see you tomorrow."

Cam shut Rachel's car door and waited while she started her engine. A smile tugged at his lips as he replayed her warm response to his kiss. She was amazing.

He'd wanted to kiss her for a long time, but it hadn't seemed right until tonight. He didn't take her affection or that kiss lightly. She was a treasure…a wonderful gift that had been entrusted to him, and he intended to tread very carefully so there was no possibility he'd hurt her.

He waved as she backed out of her parking spot and drove toward the exit. Reaching in his pocket, he found his keys, but his phone was missing. With a frown, he looked back at the building. He must have left it in his shop on the workbench. He didn't like to be without it, especially when Shannon and Eric as well as Kayla used that number to reach him.

Across the parking lot, another car engine started. A dark sedan pulled out of the shadows in the far corner. Cam's shoulders tensed. It looked like the same car he'd seen before, but he couldn't be sure. His eyes darted to Rachel's car. She turned out of the parking lot and headed north on Sixteenth. The sedan rolled across the blacktop, following Rachel's path.

Cam's gut clenched. He jogged to his SUV and jumped in, dismissing thoughts of his missing phone.

This time he would not let that guy get away.

Chapter Sixteen

Rachel drove out of the Arts Center parking lot and popped in a Carpenters' CD. The music had been a gift from her mom who loved the brother-and-sister duo since college days. Tonight seemed like the perfect time for some vintage love songs.

Strains of "Close To You" filled the car as she drove up Sixteenth Street and turned right on Harris Avenue. She touched her lips and smiled, remembering the kiss she'd shared with Cam just minutes before. That kiss, along with the way he'd talked so openly about his faith, sent a special message straight to her heart. Cam's renewed faith and caring ways made her believe she might have finally found a man she could love and trust.

Headlights flashed in her rearview mirror as they traveled over a dip in the road. Cam must have caught up and was right behind her now. Knowing he was close by, watching over her, she relaxed into the seat and hummed along with the song.

Maybe she'd invite him in for coffee when they got home. Kayla was staying overnight at Lindsey's. It would be just the two of them. Maybe they would share another kiss. Her stomach fluttered at that thought.

The house came into view. She slowed and turned in the driveway, checking the rearview mirror for Cam. But the car behind her didn't pull in, instead it rolled to a stop across the street. The headlights flashed off.

Rachel turned and looked over her shoulder. The car was a black sedan, not Cam's green SUV. She gripped the steering wheel, and her heart began to pound. *Don't panic. Just get out of the car and go inside.*

She forced herself to open the door and climb out. As she retrieved her computer bag and purse from the backseat, Cam's SUV pulled up behind the sedan.

She released the breath she had been holding. *See, you were overreacting. The driver of the sedan must be a friend of Cam's, someone he invited over.* She walked down the driveway toward the street to greet them.

Cam climbed out of his car, and even in the dim light she could see his stern expression.

"Go in the house," he shouted, then he tossed her his keys. Hard.

She caught them, but stood there staring at him, trying to make sense of what was going on.

The driver's window of the sedan powered down. A man lifted a camera, and a bright flash lit up the street.

"Hey!" Cam slammed his fist on the trunk of the sedan. "What do you think you're doing?" He strode toward the driver's door. "Who are you? What do you want?"

The sedan pealed out. Cam jumped back.

Rachel gasped. Her mind told her to turn and run, but her feet felt frozen to the sidewalk. The car raced down the street and around the corner.

Cam hustled over to her. "Do you know who that was?"

She swallowed hard, her mind spinning and her knees quivering like a bowl of Jell-O. The shadows had hidden the man's features. It might have been Kyle. But why would he take her picture? Was he trying to frighten her—prove he could find her no matter where she went? That thought struck her like a punch in the stomach, and her knees felt as if they might give way.

"Rachel?" Cam reached to steady her. "Did you recognize him?" His voice held more concern for her this time.

"No...no I didn't." That was true, but it wasn't

the whole truth. She stepped away from Cam and crossed her arms.

"Well, whoever he is, he followed you all the way from the Arts Center, and it's not the first time."

Her head jerked up. "What?"

"He followed you before, that day you left the Arts Center early so we could go shopping and fix up Kayla's room."

Her mind flashed back to that afternoon, and she remembered the strange way Cam had acted when she'd pulled in the driveway a few minutes late. "Why didn't you say something then?"

"I wasn't sure. I didn't want to scare you."

She stiffened. "Well, I'd appreciate knowing next time you suspect something like that."

He put his arm around her shoulder. "I'm sorry. I should've told you." His gentle tone soothed her for the moment. "Let's go inside," he added.

She handed him his keys, then walked with him up the porch steps, still feeling unsteady. He unlocked the door and led her into the living room. Sasha rushed forward to greet them, her tail wagging.

"Why don't you sit down? I'm going to let her outside. I'll be right back."

Rachel sunk onto the couch, closed her eyes and rubbed her temples. Would Kyle really follow her all the way up here from Seattle? How was she going to explain this to Cam? If she tried, would he believe her, or would he turn his back on her the way so many people had when they heard Kyle's accusations?

When it came to children's safety, no one wanted to take a chance. She'd been presumed guilty, and even after the charges were dropped most people didn't want to have anything to do with her. If that information ever became known here in Fairhaven, she'd lose her position as director of N.C.Y.T. for sure.

Cam returned to the living room and crossed to the couch, his stance tense. "I think we should call the police."

Panic flashed through her. "No! I don't want to do that."

He took a seat and reached for her hand. "Rachel, this is serious. He followed you home at least twice, and I'm pretty sure I've seen that same car parked at the Arts Center a few other times."

Cam's warm hand tightened around hers, but that only drove her panic deeper.

If they called the police, she'd have to tell them about the investigation in Seattle. Cam would hear the whole story, and she'd end up looking like a liar, a fool or much worse. Her stomach twisted into a tight knot. She pulled her hand away. "I don't want to get the police involved."

A tense silence stretched between them for several seconds. "Why do I get the feeling you're not telling me everything?"

Her throat burned. She got up. "I'm tired, Cam. I just want to go upstairs and go to bed."

He stood, and his piercing blue gaze pinned her in place. "I want to help you, Rachel. But I can't do that if you won't tell me what's going on."

She looked around the room trying to buy some time. She had to tell him something, but she couldn't admit her own humiliating part of the problem. "I… have an idea who it might be, but I'm not sure."

Cam tensed. "Who?"

"One of the reasons I left Seattle was because a former student was…following me."

Cam scowled. "Why didn't you tell me that before?"

"The whole thing is embarrassing. And it might not even be him."

"So…this former student have a crush on you, or was he off mentally?"

"Probably a little of both."

"Did you tell the police?"

"Yes. But he never made any verbal threats, so they told me to ignore him and pretend his skulking around didn't bother me."

Cam growled. "So it was fine with the police if he followed you around as long as he didn't say anything threatening?" He lifted his hands. "That's ridiculous!"

"They told me I could file charges against him,

but his father is a lawyer, so I didn't think I'd win. And at the time I had no job and no money to take him to court."

"So that's when you left Seattle and came to Fairhaven?"

"Yes. I thought that would put enough distance between us, and he'd leave me alone."

"So how old is he?"

"Nineteen, maybe twenty by now."

Cam frowned. "The guy in the car looked older than that." He studied her, looking unsettled.

She shifted away from him, unable to take his scrutiny any longer. She hated holding back the rest of the story, but she couldn't risk his rejection. Not tonight. "It's late. I should go."

He reached for her hand. "Rachel, wait. I'm sorry. I don't mean to give you a hard time about this. I just don't like the idea of some guy following you around." He pulled her in for a hug.

Tears burned her eyes.

Tell him the rest. Don't let your fear and pride build a wall between you.

But she pushed that thought away and hugged him tighter.

"I won't let anyone hurt you," he whispered and kissed the top of her head. "I promise."

A wave of guilt crashed over her heart. What would he say if he knew the rest of the story?

* * *

Kayla stood and gave Rachel a hug. "Thanks for letting me come up and talk to you. I really needed another woman's point of view."

Rachel held back a grin. "Any time. You're always welcome."

"Uncle Cam is great, but he just doesn't get guy-girl relationships." Her face flushed and she bit her lip. "I mean, teenage relationships. He's probably great with adult guy-girl stuff." Now her face flamed. "Oh man, I better stop before I say something really awful."

Rachel laughed. "It's okay. I understand what you mean."

"Now you can see why I have so much trouble talking to Ryan."

"Don't worry." Rachel gave Kayla a reassuring pat on the shoulder. "Just relax and be yourself."

"Okay. Thanks." She glanced at the kitchen clock. "I better go. Uncle Cam said I have to unload the dishwasher before I go over to Lindsey's. We're having a chick-flick movie night."

"Sounds fun." She followed Kayla down the steps.

At the door, Kayla turned and looked up at Rachel. "One more thing ..."

"What's that?"

"Thanks for praying for my mom. Her last test

results were a little better." Her blue eyes shone as she relayed the news.

Rachel touched Kayla's cheek. "You hold on to hope. God will carry you through this."

Kayla gave her another quick hug, then stepped out the door. "Thanks, Rachel. See you tomorrow."

"Bye, sweetie." Rachel followed her out to the side porch. She wished she could repeat her advice about being careful with her heart, but she didn't want Kayla to think she'd get a lecture each time she came to visit. Keeping the lines of communication open by doing a lot of listening seemed to be the best way to strengthen their relationship.

As Kayla trotted around the side of the house, a short bald man in a brown knit shirt and tan slacks approached the porch. He slowed and looked up at Rachel.

Apprehension prickled along Rachel's arms. Less than twenty-four hours ago, she'd realized someone was stalking her again. This man didn't look threatening, but she didn't recognize him.

He stopped at the bottom of the steps. "Rachel Clark?"

She straightened. "Yes?"

"My name is Allen Thayer. I'm a private investigator." He mounted the porch steps, pulled a card from his pocket and handed it to her.

She glanced at the card, confirming his name

and occupation. His Chicago address sent a wave of uncertainty through her. "What can I do for you?"

"I've been hired by John Harding to search for his daughter, Rose Marie Harding."

Rachel narrowed her eyes. "I don't know anyone by either of those names."

"You might not remember him, but I believe John Harding is your father."

The shocking words hit Rachel like a jolt of electricity. She grabbed the porch rail. "What?"

"Birth records show your name was originally Rose Marie Harding. It was changed to Rachel Marie Clark just before your third birthday after your mother moved from Chicago to Seattle and divorced your father."

"How do you know that?"

He cocked his head. "Ms. Clark, I'm a private investigator. That's what we do."

An idea flashed into her mind. She glanced past him to the street where a dark sedan sat parked at the curb. "You're the one who's been following me."

The cockiness faded from his expression. "I'm sorry about last night. I didn't mean to upset you or your boyfriend."

She ignored his comment about Cam. "Why did you take my picture?"

"I told your father I was certain I'd found you. But he wanted to see a photo first."

"You sent him my picture? What did he say?"

A slight grin returned to Thayer's face. "He said, 'She looks just like her mother, but she's got my eyes.'"

Rachel gasped. "I don't believe this."

"I assure you it's the truth. Your father's been searching for you for quite a while."

Confusing thoughts tumbled through her mind. "What does he want?"

"He wrote a letter explaining everything." Thayer pulled an envelope from his pocket and held it out to her.

Her fingers trembled as she took it.

"Don't worry. He has good intentions. I wouldn't take the case if he didn't." With that, he turned and walked down the steps. At the bottom, he stopped and looked over his shoulder. "I'd say this is your lucky day, Ms. Clark."

She leaned against the railing for support. How could this be true? Her father was an angry, dangerous man who had a serious drinking problem and a heavy-handed approach to getting his way. At least that was what her mother had always said.

Rachel had convinced herself it was better not to know a man like that. Yet, in a secret corner of her heart, she'd always longed to know he loved her enough to come and find her.

Now that she held his letter in her hands, she didn't know if she had the courage to open it.

* * *

Cam poured himself a glass of iced tea and set the pitcher back in the refrigerator. The front screen door slammed, and a few seconds later Kayla trooped into the kitchen.

"So, you and Rachel have a good visit?"

"Yeah." The tense lines around Kayla's eyes and mouth had disappeared, and her mood seemed much brighter.

Having Rachel upstairs had worked out so much better than he'd ever imagined. Her input in Kayla's life was priceless, and he certainly liked having her close by. He grinned and took a sip of his tea. "Hey, did you return that sweater you borrowed from her?"

"Oh, sorry. I forgot." Kayla popped the dishwasher door and lifted out the utensil rack.

Cam downed the last of his tea. "That's okay. I'll run it up to her."

"Maybe you should wait. I think she's got company."

He frowned slightly. "Oh yeah, who?"

"Some guy I've never seen before."

Cam tensed, and his frown deepened.

Kayla grinned. "Don't worry, Uncle Cam. I don't think he's gonna steal her heart. He didn't look like her type at all."

Cam headed toward the back door. "I'll be back in a few minutes."

An uneasy feeling urged him on as he hustled around the house. He spotted Rachel sitting on her top porch step, alone. "Kayla said you had a visitor. Everything okay?"

She blinked and looked up at him, her face pale. "I…I don't know."

Cam sat down next to her. "Who was it?"

She released a shuddering breath. "A private detective who was hired by…my father. He's the one who's been following me. He gave me this letter." She looked down at the envelope in her hands.

"Wow. What does it say?"

"I don't know. I'm afraid to open it."

Cam's heart twisted, and he put his arm around her shoulders. "Hey, it's gonna be okay."

She brushed a tear from the corner of her eye. "I don't know why I'm crying. I should be happy. But this all just came out of the blue. I had no idea he was looking for me." She pulled in a sharp breath and turned to him. "What if he wants to meet me?"

He tucked a strand of her silky hair behind her ear. "Just take it one step at a time." He nodded toward the letter. "Why don't you open it and see what he says?"

She fiddled with the envelope a moment more, then tore it open and pulled out the letter. "'Dear Rose,'" she read aloud.

"Wait, why is he calling you Rose?"

"Apparently, that was my name until my mom changed it."

"Okay. Go ahead."

"'I am thrilled this letter has finally reached you. Even though we have been apart for many years, you have always been on mind and in my heart. I've missed you very much, and I hope, now that you are grown, we will have an opportunity to get to know each other again.'" Emotion choked off her voice.

His heart clenched, watching her. "You want me to read it?"

"No. I want to do it." She cleared her throat and started again.

"'I am sorry for all the pain and heartache I caused you and your mother. Thinking back and remembering how I treated you both is one of the biggest sorrows of my life. I was young, foolish and selfish, and I lacked the character and courage I needed to deal with my out-of-control drinking and abusive behavior. Losing you and your mother was a terrible blow, but it took three more years before I finally admitted my problems and asked for help.

"'By God's grace and with the help of my friends at AA, I have been clean and sober for twenty years. I married a wonderful, caring woman named Nina eighteen years ago. We have a son, Jason, seventeen, and a daughter Courtney, fifteen. They are great kids who are doing well and making their old dad proud.

"'I worked in construction for a number of years, and now have my own company with more than forty employees. We build retail and office buildings all over Chicago.

"'Though I have had a good life, not knowing where you were or what was happening in your life has been very hard for me. I have searched for you several times over the years, hoping and praying I would find you.

"'I would love to hear how you are doing, and if you are willing, I would like to start rebuilding our relationship. But the choice is up to you. I will understand if you decide not to contact me. But I am hoping and praying you will.

"'With love from your father, John Harding'"

She released a trembling breath, her gaze still focused on the letter.

Cam gently rubbed her shoulder. "So what do you think?"

"He certainly seems different than the way my mom always described him."

"Sounds like he's changed a lot since you and your mom left."

She folded the letter, her face an unreadable mask.

"So…are you going to call him?"

She slipped the letter in the envelope. "I want to talk to my mom first."

Cam scanned her face. "You don't need her permission to contact your dad. You're an adult."

Her expression tightened. "I know. But she's the one who raised me. She's been there for me all these years. I think I owe it to her to listen to her perspective."

Disappointment coursed through Cam. "You are going to call him, though, aren't you, after you talk to your mom?"

She pushed off from the step and stood. "How do I know if he's telling the truth? Maybe he made all this up."

"Why would he do that?" Cam stood and faced her. "He's obviously sorry for the way he treated you, and he's trying to make up for it."

"Why are you defending him?"

"I'm not, I just think your emotions might be clouding the picture a little."

She crossed her arms and turned away, but not before he saw the hurt in her eyes.

He touched her shoulder. "I'm trying to help. I don't mean to push."

"Well, you are pushing, and I don't appreciate it."

He was quiet for a few seconds. "I'm sorry, but it reminds me of what happened between me and my dad."

She glanced over her shoulder. "What do you mean?"

"About three months before he died, we had a big argument. The next day my dad called, but I wouldn't answer. I wanted to punish him for confronting me, and show him I was old enough to make my own choices. Then he wrote me a letter and apologized. But I didn't return his calls or answer the letter. In fact, I never spoke to him again." He stopped and swallowed, still feeling the terrible weight of that decision. "Then he died, and it was too late to tell him I was sorry and that I loved him."

He took her hand. "Don't make that same mistake. I know it seems like a huge risk to put your heart on the line and contact him, but think about what you could gain if he really is the man he says in that letter."

Tears pooled in her eyes, and her chin trembled.

"Call him and work things out while you've got the chance."

She pulled away. "You have no idea what his choices cost me or my mom, or the pain we had to live with for all these years. So don't tell me what to do." She dashed into her apartment and jerked the door closed behind her.

Cam stared at the curtain swaying in the window of the door, then blew out a deep breath. She obviously wasn't ready to talk to her father. Why had he pushed so hard? It probably had more to do with his own need to work through his issues with his father, than it had to do with helping Rachel.

He leaned on the porch railing and bowed his head. *Father, please help Rachel think this through and make the right choice. Help her forgive her father. Show me what I ought to do. And if there's any way You can get a message to my dad, would You tell him I'm sorry, and that I love him?*

Chapter Seventeen

Rachel wearily rubbed her forehead and trudged up the aisle of the auditorium. The headache that had been building all morning began pounding out a painful rhythm in the back of her head.

The kids had an unbelievable amount of energy for a Monday morning. Their antics during the last three hours had stolen her last ounce of patience. Thankfully, most of the younger ones were heading home, and she would only have to deal with a dozen or so cast members at the afternoon rehearsal.

It didn't help that's she'd barely slept last night. Between her troubled thoughts about contacting her father, and her regret over lashing out at Cam, she felt like a wet washcloth being twisted and wrung out to dry.

She pushed open the door to the auditorium and glanced down the hall toward Cam's frame shop. His door stood open and a warm light glowed within.

She ought to walk down there and apologize, but she couldn't face him right now. Maybe after lunch she'd work up the courage.

But what would she say? The first thing he'd ask was, had she contacted her father. When she said no, he'd be disappointed in her all over again.

She turned away and walked into her office. Dropping her clipboard on her desk, she deflated into her chair. What a mess! Closing her eyes, she laid her head back and tried to relax the tight muscles in her neck. The sound of heels clicking on the tile floor reached her. She lifted her head and look toward the door.

Melanie strode in carrying a file folder. "I need to speak to you." Her voice grated on Rachel's nerves like fingernails clawing down a chalkboard.

Rachel winced. "I have a killer headache. Can it wait 'til later?"

Melanie's jaw jutted forward. "No. It can't."

"Look, I'm sorry the kids were rowdy in the halls this morning. Chandra wasn't feeling well, so I sent her home. Amy and I had to split the group, and she's not used to handling that many kids."

Melanie opened her mouth to reply.

But Rachel cut her off. "I promise I'll keep them quieter tomorrow."

"I'm not here to talk about the kids."

Oh, great. If she says one more word about Cam and me, I am going to scream.

"Did you live in Seattle before you moved here?"

Rachel eased forward. "Yes."

"Were you a teacher at Roosevelt High?"

Her stomach tensed. "Why do you want to know?"

"I knew there must be more to your story, so I did a little research, and look what I found." A triumphant gleam lit up Melanie's eyes. She pulled a copy of a newspaper article from the folder and slid it across Rachel's desk.

The headline read, Roosevelt Teacher Accused of Inappropriate Relationship with Student.

Rachel sucked in a sharp breath. "That's not true."

"It's right there in black and white." Melanie narrowed her eyes and scanned the article. "'The investigation suggests Ms. Clark demonstrated a lack of professional judgment, and if the accusations are proven true, they are grounds for dismissal.'"

Rachel clenched her jaw, fighting the urge to rip the article from her hand.

"Did you lose your job over this?"

"Yes...but it was a complicated situation. That article doesn't begin to tell what really happened."

"I'd rather not hear the sordid details."

Rachel jumped up. "That's not what I meant."

"I can't believe you have the nerve to move here

and work with kids when you have this kind of background."

"You don't know anything about me or my background."

"I know enough, and I won't stand by and let you endanger those children."

"I am not a danger to anyone"

"Well, here's the way I see it. You have a choice to make. Either you resign as director of N.C.Y.T., or I'll tell Cam and all the parents what happened in Seattle."

Rachel gasped. "You're not serious."

"I am."

Rachel walked around the desk. "But the summer musical is only three weeks away. Think about the kids!"

"That is exactly who I am thinking about."

"Those charges are based on lies!"

The hateful gleam in Melanie's eyes spoke louder than her words.

"You don't care if this is true or not. You're just jealous of my relationship with Cam."

Melanie wrinkled her nose. "He won't want anything to do with you when he hears about this."

"You're wrong. He'll stand up for me."

"I wouldn't count on it. He has his own reputation to think about, and he has to look out for his niece. Once this comes out, it will be the end of your relationship."

All the strength drained from Rachel's legs, and she leaned back against her desk. "Please, Melanie, don't do this. So many people will be hurt."

She leveled her cold gaze at Rachel. "You have until Friday to make a decision. Resign, or I contact the parents."

Rachel clenched her fists. "I'm not resigning!"

The blonde spun on her heel and strode out the door.

Rachel slumped into her chair and lowered her head to her hands. What was she going to do now?

Cam gripped the phone tighter, counting the rings as he waited for his sister to pick up. Looking out the kitchen window, he watched Kayla and her friend, Lindsey, squirting each other with the hose. They were supposed to be washing the SUV, but he didn't mind the impromptu water fight. Seeing Kayla laugh and enjoy time with her friend was worth a few more dollars on his water bill.

After six rings, Shannon's voice mail came on, telling him to leave a message. He blew out a deep breath, hoping to drain the frustration from his tone. "Hey, Shannon. Sorry I missed your call. Hope everything is okay. We'll be home all evening. Try again when you get this message. If I don't hear from you in a couple hours, I'll call you back. Take care. Bye."

Cam dropped his phone in his pocket. Shannon

hadn't sounded upset when she left her message, but he couldn't be sure. Every few days she shared some test result or conversation with the doctor that either raised their hopes, or left them anxious and wondering what would happen next.

He glanced outside at Rachel's empty parking spot and his mood dropped a few more points. She'd been avoiding him since Sunday evening when the P.I. showed up with that letter from her father. Pushing her to call had been a bad move. Maybe he should call her now.

He reached for his phone, then slowly withdrew his hand from his pocket. She'd made it clear Sunday night—she needed more time to process this huge shift in her world.

But not seeing her for three days had left him feeling unsettled and distracted. He couldn't stop thinking about her. His focus was shot.

He yanked opened the refrigerator and grabbed the plate of hamburger patties.

A car pulled in the driveway. He glanced outside as Rachel's Toyota rolled to a stop next to his SUV. Kayla dropped the hose and ran to greet her. Rachel climbed out of the car. Lindsey grabbed the hose and sprayed Kayla's feet. His niece squealed and ran to hide behind Rachel.

Cam snatched the barbeque sauce off the counter and headed out the back door. Maybe an invitation to dinner would ease the strain between them. The screen door slammed behind him. Rachel looked up. He smiled and waved.

She slowly lifted her hand, but her smile didn't reach her eyes.

His stomach clenched. He must have done more damage with his comments on Sunday night than he realized. He crossed the patio and tried to shake off his concern. Maybe she was just tired or stressed about the situation with her father. But as he stationed himself at the grill, she stayed in the driveway talking to Kayla and Lindsey.

Apparently, she was in no hurry to see him. "Fine," he muttered, then turned away and hit the ignition switch on the grill.

So what was her problem? They'd had disagreements before, and she'd always been willing to work them out. What was different this time? It wasn't his fault she had a long-lost father who hired a P.I. to find her. Why couldn't she see that as good news?

Two seconds later he grimaced at his selfish thoughts. It might help if he tried to see things from her perspective. Adjusting to the news her father wanted to be a part of her life again was obviously a huge challenge for her.

Pride was a hard pill to swallow, but Rachel was worth it. He pulled in a deep breath and crossed the patio to meet her. "Hey." He held up his spatula. "We're grilling burgers. Would you like to join us?"

"Thanks, but...I've got a lot to do this evening."

He tried not to let her rebuff sting, but it did. "Why don't you go up and work for a while. I'll give you a call when we're ready." He leaned closer. "Besides, I could use some sane adult conversation tonight."

She took a step back. "I wouldn't be good company. I've got a headache."

He searched her face, noting the gray half circles under her eyes and the tightness around her mouth. "Sorry to hear that. I'll run a burger up to you then."

She tilted her head and looked at him with a sad smile. "You don't have to do that."

"You've got to eat. Why don't you take something for the headache and lie down for a while. I'll leave your dinner in the kitchen for later."

Her eyes filled as she reached up and touched the side of his face. "Thanks. That's sweet."

He swallowed. Oh, man. If she started crying, that would totally do him in.

But she turned away and headed across the patio.

She probably did have a headache and work to do, but there was more going on behind that sad smile than she was telling him. He felt like a wall separated them...and he didn't like that feeling at all.

* * *

Rachel slowly climbed the stairs to her second-floor apartment. Each step felt like she was dragging huge weights tied around her ankles. The pounding in her head increased, turning her stomach into a queasy mess.

When she reached the top landing she dropped her computer case and purse on the side table and headed for the bathroom. She took two pain relievers and drank a tall glass of water. Gazing at her reflection on the mirror, she slowly shook her head. *You look as terrible as you feel. And it's no wonder. Your foolish mistakes are about to destroy N.C.Y.T. and break the hearts of fifty kids!*

With a weary sigh she walked into her bedroom and flopped down on the bed. Staring at her ceiling fan, her thoughts swirled like a tornado. Hot tears slipped from the corners of her eyes and dripped into her ears.

Please, God, I need Your help. I've tried to figure this out on my own, but that's only gotten me in deeper trouble. Please show me what to do. I'm ready to listen to whatever You say.

Closing her eyes, she slowed her breathing and waited for His answer. A sense of calm settled over her, and she began to think more clearly.

This had all started because she had tried to hide her past mistakes rather than admitting them, starting with Suzanne at the job interview. Oh, she'd told her she'd been falsely accused by a student and had resigned because of it, but she hadn't mentioned how her foolish decision to ignore her school's policy and meet Kyle off campus had compounded the problem and called her judgment into question. That was a humbling bridge she still needed to cross.

She'd also have to tell Suzanne about Melanie's threat to leak the article to the parents. If Suzanne was supportive they could face the parents together, and there was a slim possibility they could avoid a catastrophe. There were a lot of ifs and maybes in that line of thinking, but she knew total honesty was the only pathway out of these problems.

The sound of Cam's voice and then Kayla and Lindsey's laughter drifted up from the back patio.

She closed her eyes and swallowed. Cam deserved to know the truth, too, all of it. She needed to tell him what led up to the accusations and give him details about the investigation and her resignation. Her stomach churned as she imagined his reaction. But how could she expect to build a strong and trusting relationship with him if she wasn't willing to admit her mistakes and share her weaknesses?

If only she had told him the truth from the beginning, but she'd had no idea they would grow to care about each other the way they did. Would those feelings be enough to hold them together? Would he forgive her, or would this end their relationship as Melanie hoped?

Staring at the swirling fan, she made her decision. She got up, retrieved her phone, sat on the side of her bed and bowed her head. *Lord, please give me the courage.*

Pressing her lips together, she flipped it open and punched in his number. It rang twice and his voice-mail message played, postponing the inevitable.

She had to force her voice to cooperate. "Hi, this is Rachel. I need to talk to you about something, but I don't want to do it in front of Kayla. Could you come up and see me later? Or I can come down. Just call me, okay? It's important."

Cam flipped the last burger onto the platter. His phone vibrated in his pocket. He checked the ID and lifted it to his ear. "Hey, how is my favorite sister?"

"I'm your only sister, and I'm doing okay." The smile in her voice reassured him this wasn't a crisis call.

He released a deep breath. "Good. What's up?"

"I was hoping you could help me with something."

"Sure. What is it?"

"There was a freak windstorm in Seattle last night. A tree limb broke off and crashed into our garage roof."

Cam frowned and placed the platter on the patio table. "How bad is it?"

"I'm not sure. One of our elderly neighbors called, but she's hard of hearing, so we couldn't get the whole story. Could you and Kayla drive down and check it out? All of Eric's tools are on that side of the garage, and they're predicting more rain tomorrow. He thought maybe you could put a tarp over that area."

"Okay. We'll head down there after dinner."

"Great. I called the insurance agent and gave him your cell number. He said he'd come by in the morning and take a look. Do you think you could stay over and talk to him?"

"Sure. Don't worry about it. I'll give you a call after we see what's going on. Then we'll talk to the insurance guy and make a plan to get it fixed."

"Thanks, Cam. You're a lifesaver."

He grinned. "Butterscotch or cherry?"

She laughed. "Very funny. Can I talk to Kayla?"

"Sure. I'll call you later." He passed the phone to his niece and turned off the grill. Shannon sounded good, almost like her old self. A surge of hope lifted some of the weight he had been carrying. *Please, God, bring her through this storm.*

Cam poured a glass of iced tea for each of them while he listened to Kayla tell Shannon a funny story about play rehearsal. He glanced up at Rachel's window. His trip to Seattle would squelch his hope of spending time with her tonight. But at least he could follow through on his promise to bring her dinner. He loaded a burger on a plate, then added a dill pickle, potato chips and fruit salad the girls had made. He'd take it up to her after he changed. He'd also let her know he planned to be away overnight. Hopefully, by the time he got back tomorrow, she'd feel better and be ready to let him back into her world.

Twenty minutes later he climbed the stairs to Rachel's apartment. Stopping on the landing, he called her name, but she didn't answer. He set the foil-wrapped dinner on the counter in the kitchen and glanced around. The sink was empty except for one coffee cup, and the counters were neat and clear. He walked out to the landing.

Rachel's bedroom door stood open. He walked over and peeked in. His steps stalled in the doorway, and a slow smile lifted his lips. She lay on top of the comforter, eyes closed, curled up in a ball, still dressed in the same clothes she'd been wearing when she came home. She hadn't even taken off her sandals. Poor girl must be exhausted, but she'd never looked sweeter.

Her relaxed expression and steady breathing assured him she was sound asleep. The ceiling fan rotated overhead, spreading a light breeze around the room, but the temperature would drop when the sun set in a couple hours. He quietly crossed the room, took the light blanket off the trunk at the foot of her bed and laid it over her. With a gentle hand, he tucked it lightly around her shoulders.

She stirred for a moment. He stilled, hoping he wouldn't wake her. When her breathing returned to its slow, steady pattern, he bent and placed a feather-light kiss on the forehead. *Sweet dreams, Rachel. I'll be counting the hours 'til I see you again.*

With one last glance, he slipped out the door.

Chapter Eighteen

Raindrops pelted Cam's head and shoulders as he climbed the ladder leaning against the side of Eric and Shannon's garage. The tarp he and Kayla had stretched over the hole in the roof last night had come loose and now flapped in the gusty wind.

Cam gripped the sides of the ladder and glanced down at Kayla. "Hold it steady."

She looked up, squinting against the rain. Water splashed in her face and ran off the hood of her yellow raincoat. "I am, but hurry up. I'm getting soaked."

"You're not the only one!" he shouted, then sent her a teasing grin. He didn't mind this little adventure. In fact, fighting against the storm to take care of this problem for his family gave him an adrenalin rush.

When he reached the rooftop, he stopped to brush the water from his eyes and scope out the situation.

Balancing on one foot, he leaned across the roof, grabbed the tarp and hammered in the first nail.

Kayla's cell phone rang. He glanced over the side in time to see her turn around and sit on a lower rung of the ladder. She flipped open the phone and lifted it to her ear.

That girl and her phone! You'd think she could do without it for a few minutes, especially in the middle of a storm. He huffed and turned back to the roof. But, he had to admit, her phone had come in handy since he'd left his behind by mistake when he changed into his work pants.

The howling wind and pounding raindrops snatched away the first part of Kayla's conversation. Then she screamed.

Cam's foot slipped, he gasped and grabbed the ladder. "What's going on?" he yelled.

She waved him off as though she was having a hard time hearing the person on the other end of the line. The wind died down a little as he pounded in the last nail.

"I can't believe it! Are you sure?" Kayla's high-pitched voice carried a note of panic. "Well…what did Ryan say?"

More teenage drama. Cam shook his head. "I'm coming down."

"Text it to me. I've got to go." She pocketed her phone, then spun around and looked up at him. "Haley's mom is pulling her out of the play!"

Cam clambered down and jumped to the ground. "How come?"

"She said Rachel got fired from her last job for doing something really bad with a student."

Cam pulled in a sharp breath. "That's not true."

"That's what I said." Kayla's phone chirped, and she flipped it open. "Haley is texting me the link."

"What link?" Cam led her back toward the house. "You girls need to stop spreading rumors or someone is going to get hurt."

"Haley only told me and Lindsey."

"Oh great." Lindsey was an outgoing kid with a ton of friends. He couldn't imagine her keeping anything to herself for very long.

"Haley said there's an article about it in the Seattle paper." Kayla strode into the family room and turned on the computer. Her fingers flew over the keys as she typed in the link.

Cam crossed his arms and scowled at the screen. This had to be some kind of mix-up. Rachel would never do anything to hurt a student. She loved kids. Making sure they were safe and well supervised was important to her.

The *Seattle Times* banner popped up on the screen, and then the article headline appeared: Roosevelt Teacher Accused of Inappropriate Relationship with Student.

Cam's gut clenched, and he spun Kayla's chair around. "I don't want you reading that."

Her eyes flashed. "I'm not a child. I need to know what's going on."

"Just give me a second." He clamped his jaw, forced his gaze past her shoulder and read the first paragraph. His hands clenched as he scanned the shocking words.

How could this be true? Rachel had high moral standards and good character. At least that was what she had led him and everyone else to believe. Was that all a lie? Had she fooled them all?

"Well? Can I read it now?"

He blinked and shifted his gaze to Kayla. Everything in him wanted to protect his niece from this information. But all the kids would be talking about it soon. It might be better for her to read the article while she was with him. "All right." He let go of her chair.

She spun around and leaned forward, her shoulders tense and her gaze focused on the computer screen. She gasped and then slowly shook her head. Finally, she turned and looked up at him. Tears glistened in her deep blue eyes. "Did you know? Did she tell you?"

His eyes burned, and he tried to swallow, but it felt like a boulder was stuck in his throat. "No. No she didn't."

Chandra leaned closer to Rachel. "I don't see how we're going to rehearse the second act without Haley and Kayla."

Rachel's stomach tensed. She glanced at the stage where the rest of the cast stood in small clusters talking and waiting to begin. With only a little more than two weeks until their first performance, having all the cast members present was vital.

A worried frown creased Chandra's forehead. "It's not like Haley to miss a rehearsal and not call. Something must be wrong."

Rachel pulled her phone from her pocket. "I'll call her again." But she'd already called twice, and no one had answered.

At least Kayla had left a message this morning and explained her absence—something about a tree falling through their garage roof in Seattle. She hoped to be back in Fairhaven by mid-afternoon and would come to rehearsal as soon as she and Cam returned.

Why had the call come from Kayla rather than Cam? Didn't he care that she had something important to tell him? Dealing with a tree through his sister's garage roof might take some time, but didn't he have five minutes to call her back?

After the tenth ring, Rachel huffed and snapped her phone shut. Haley was not answering. The rehearsal would have to go on without her. She turned to Chandra. "You'll have to play Anne, and Lindsey can stand in for Kayla."

Chandra lifted her brows. "Are you sure?" Her

tone suggested she thought Rachel was one step away from crazy.

"Do you have a better idea?"

Chandra winced. "Not really." She turned and trotted up the steps to the stage. "All right. We've got a show to rehearse."

Rachel took a seat in the front row and tried to ignore the sense of foreboding hovering over her.

Two and a half hours later she stood at the front of the auditorium and released a weary sigh. "Okay, everyone let's gather round." She motioned the cast over, and they took seats with their legs dangling over the front of the stage.

"Good work. I know today was a challenge without Haley and Kayla, but I'm proud of each of you for giving it your best effort."

The mood of the whole group seemed to be dragging, and they exchanged doubtful glances.

"So what's up with Haley?" Ryan crossed his arms, clearly perturbed that his costar had skipped rehearsal. "Where is she?"

"I'm not sure, but I intend to find out. When we accept a role, we make a commitment to the whole cast, and it's important to—"

The auditorium doors swung open, and Haley's mother, Gail Mitchell, marched down the aisle. Her stern expression was mirrored on the faces of the four other parents who followed her.

Rachel froze. Something was wrong, and she had a terrible hunch she knew what it might be.

Cam walked in a few steps behind them with Kayla at his side.

Rachel's breath caught in her throat. What was he doing with this hostile group?

Cam's penetrating gaze connected with Rachel's for a split second, then shifted away. Kayla hurried down the aisle with him, her wide-eyed look scanning the cast and then settling on Rachel.

"Ms. Clark, we'd like to have a word with you," Gail Mitchell announced.

Rachel's face burned, but she lifted her chin and forced her voice to remain calm. "Of course."

"Not in front of the children," Gabriel's father added, his silver brows furrowed.

A heavy blanket of dread dropped over her shoulders. She clenched her jaw and turned to Chandra. "Take the kids out to the hallway. They can wait for their parents there."

"What's going on?" Chandra whispered.

"I'll let you know as soon as I'm done here." She tried to use a reassuring tone, but it probably sounded more like a cry for help.

"You sure you don't want me to stay?"

"I'll be all right. Go ahead and take the kids out."

Chandra nodded, still looking worried, then gathered the cast and led them past the parents.

"I want you to go with them." Cam nodded to Kayla.

She gave her head a defiant shake. "I'm staying."

Cam straightened. "You need to go, now." His firm tone left her no option.

With a wild flash of her eyes, Kayla spun away and marched off with Ryan and the others.

Rachel's heart sunk as she watched them go. Facing these accusations again would be difficult, but she'd do anything to avoid hurting these kids. Maybe there was still a chance to salvage this situation. She leveled her gaze at Gail Mitchell. "We missed Haley at rehearsal today. I'd appreciate a call next time."

"There won't be a next time. Haley is not going to be in the play."

Rachel clenched her jaw, her anger building. It was one thing to question her, it was another to pull Haley out and ruin the summer musical for all the kids. "I don't see how I can replace her at this point."

"We're not just talking about Haley. None of our children are going to be a part of this production as long as you're the director."

Shockwaves rippled through her. "What?

Several parents exchanged uncomfortable glances.

Gail raised her chin. "We know what happened in Seattle, how you were fired from your job because you were…romantically involved with one of your students."

Fire seared through her. "That is not true!"

All the parents began to talk at once: "How can you say that?" "We read the article online!" "Well, what did happen with that boy then?" "How can we trust you to work with our kids?"

As their rapid-fire questions filled the air, Rachel looked past them at Cam. Though he was silent, chilling doubts filled his eyes. Her heart dropped to her toes. What a fool she'd been to believe he would defend her.

She held up her hand and quieted the group. "I promise you, there is an explanation for all of this, and I'll answer all your questions, but not here, and not now."

Another round of angry comments rose from the group. "Why not?" "We came here for answers!" "What are you trying to hide?"

"I want to meet with *all* the parents at the same time so this information won't have to be passed on by anyone else. As I'm sure you're all aware, rumors and gossip can do a lot of damage." She took a moment to make eye contact with each parent. "I'd like to be sure that doesn't happen in this case."

Lindsey's mom blinked, looking apologetic. "I can call the other parents and set up a meeting. It's too late to try and reach everyone for tonight, but we could probably get the word out for tomorrow."

"All right. Tomorrow night, seven o'clock, here in the auditorium. Is that agreeable to everyone?" Rachel glanced around the group.

Several parents nodded, but Gail's expression remained defiant. "We won't be sending our kids to drama camp or rehearsal until this is settled." Her mouth puckered in a determined line. "And if we're not happy with your *explanation,* then we expect a full refund on the drama camp fees."

Cold dread flowed through Rachel. She gripped the folds of her skirt. There was no way she could give a refund to anyone. The money had been spent on salaries, costumes, props and set-construction materials for the musical.

The parents spoke to each other in hushed tones as they walked out of the auditorium. But Cam stood about ten feet away, watching her.

She grabbed her clipboard off the chair and headed toward the other aisle.

"So you're just going to walk away?" He strode after her.

She fought back her tears as she turned around. "What do you want me to do?"

"I want you to tell me what's going on."

She swallowed and steadied her voice. "I already told you—I'll answer everyone's questions tomorrow night."

"But I'm not everyone."

She lifted her hand to her forehead, shielding her

eyes from his intense gaze. "I am so tired of having to defend myself against these charges."

"Maybe if you'd told me about them before, I would've been standing up there with you, instead of back here wondering what to believe."

His words snatched her breath away, and she dropped her hand. "I'm sorry, Cam. I didn't think the problems from Seattle would follow me here."

"Well they have, so don't you think it's time you told me the rest of the story."

She had planned to do just that, but it would've been a whole lot easier if he hadn't ignored her phone message and then showed up with Gail Mitchell and her gang.

But she'd prayed for direction and a way out of all this trouble. God's answer last night seemed to be, tell Cam the truth, so she needed to follow through and trust she'd heard God clearly.

"Remember me telling you about the student who was following me?"

Cam nodded, silently urging her on with his eyes.

"I thought he was just a mixed-up kid from a troubled family who needed someone to talk to, so I tried to befriend him. Then one day he was really upset, and he hinted he was thinking about suicide. He asked me to meet him at a coffee shop after school. I knew it was risky, but I agreed. I thought I could convince him to get professional help, but he

misread my concern and confessed he had feelings
for me. I had no idea that was coming. I tried to let
him down as gently as possible, but he was angry.

"Someone saw us there, and the word got around
school. A few days later he was called in to the
principal's office. Maybe he felt cornered, or maybe
he just wanted to get back at me, but whatever the
reason, he lied about what happened, and the whole
thing blew up in my face."

She'd avoided looking at him as she told the story,
but now she lifted her gaze, longing to read understanding in his eyes.

But shadows darkened his gaze, and a frown
creased his forehead. "So there was nothing going
on between you and this student?"

"Nothing…just a teacher trying to help a hurting
young man."

"Then why did you lose your job?"

"Anytime they suspect something like that, there
has to be an investigation. I had to take a leave of
absence, and by the time the investigation was over,
so many people believed the lies, there was no way
I could continue teaching at Roosevelt."

"Did he ever confess?"

"No, but he kept changing his story, and that made
the police suspicious. The lawyer for the teachers'
union convinced them to drop the charges, but I had
to resign. There was no other choice."

He sighed and shook his head, doubt filling his eyes.

She pulled in a sharp breath. "You don't believe me?"

"I didn't say that. I'm just trying to figure out why you never said anything before now, especially when we were trying to figure out who was following you."

"Can't you see why I didn't want to tell you? The way I handled everything made it worse. I never should've met with him outside of school. I should've gone straight to the administration. But I convinced myself I was the only one who could help him. That was prideful and foolish, and it ended up costing me my job and my reputation."

Cam crossed his arms, his stern expression unchanged.

Hot tears filled her eyes. Her honest confession didn't make any difference to him. He would never defend someone he didn't believe. She spun away and fled out the side door.

Cam charged up the steps to Ross's apartment and banged on his front door. He waited two seconds, then banged again. Where was his friend when he needed him?

"All right, all right. I'm coming." Ross opened the door. "You're gonna knock a hole in it if you hit it any harder."

Cam pushed past him. "I need to talk to you."

"Okay, why don't you come in...but since you're already in, have a seat."

Cam paced to the other side of the room. "Can't sit. Not now."

Ross pushed his glasses up his nose. "What's the problem?"

"Rachel's in big trouble."

Ross's irritated expression melted away. "What happened?"

"You got Internet?"

"Sure." Ross left the room and a few seconds later brought back his laptop. He sat on the couch and opened his computer. "Here you go."

Cam took a seat, typed in the link to the *Seattle Times* and searched for the article. "Look at this." He turned the computer toward his friend.

Ross scanned the words, and his dark eyes took on a stormy cast. "That's got to be someone else. Rachel would never get involved with a seventeen-year-old kid."

Cam's gut twisted again. "Oh, it's her all right."

Ross pulled back. "No way!"

"She says the kid lied." Cam repeated a shortened version of Rachel's story. "Some of the parents found out about it and confronted her after rehearsal today. They're pulling their kids out of the program, and they want their money back from drama camp."

"What's she going to do?

"She set up a meeting for tomorrow night and said she'd tell them what happened, but I don't know if she'll be able to save her job or the drama program."

"Oh, man, this stinks! She should sue that kid or his family."

Cam shook his head. "I don't know."

"Why not? Look at all the trouble he caused with his lies."

Cam glared at the computer screen, turning the story over in his mind.

"Wait a minute." Ross narrowed his eyes. "You believe her, don't you?"

Cam shifted under his friend's scrutiny. "I don't know. That's why I'm here."

Ross gripped Cam's shoulder. "Listen to me. You know Rachel. She's the real deal. If she says the kid lied, then that's what happened."

Cam rubbed his forehead, trying to wrap his mind around his conflicting thoughts. He wanted to believe her, but everything made her look guilty.

"Think about everything she's done for Kayla—giving her a scholarship to drama camp and spending all that time with her. Didn't you say if Rachel hadn't helped you figure out how to deal with Kayla, you'd have been sunk?"

Cam grimaced and got up. "Yeah, I did. But if she's not guilty, then why did she keep it all a secret?" He smacked his palm against the fireplace mantel.

"That's what's really bugging me. Why didn't she tell me about this before now?"

"She was probably afraid you wouldn't believe her." Ross looked at Cam over the top of his dark-framed glasses. "And I'd say her fears were not too far off the mark."

Cam closed his eyes and groaned. "Oh, brother, I made a royal mess of this whole thing, didn't I?"

Ross crossed the room and stood beside him. "You got that right. So what are you going to do about it?"

Cam rubbed his forehead. "I'm not sure."

"Well, Rachel needs you more than ever, so you better figure it out."

Chapter Nineteen

Rachel gripped the cool metal railing of the fire escape and stared across the Arts Center parking lot, while the mind-numbing events of the last twenty minutes tumbled through her mind. A cold shiver raced up her back, though it was a warm evening, and only a slight breeze stirred the branches of the nearby fir trees.

The heavy metal door leading into the auditorium squeaked open behind her. Her breath caught, and she closed her eyes. Was it Cam? Had he come to apologize? Would he take her in his arms and say he believed her?

"Rachel?" Chandra moved to her side. "Are you all right?"

Rachel's shoulders sagged. "I feel like I've been run over by a Mack truck—twice."

"Ahh, Rachel, I'm sorry, but it's going to be

okay." Chandra rubbed a comforting circle on Rachel's back.

"You might not think so when I tell you why those parents were here."

"I already heard. As soon as I took the kids out to the hallway, Lindsey burst into tears and told everyone about the article online and how Haley's mom wants to pull her out of the show."

Rachel moaned and covered her face. "You mean all the kids know?"

"Yep. And you should've heard them defending you. We all know there has to be more to the story than what they read online."

Rachel's nose stung. "Thank you for believing in me. That means a lot. But I'm not sure everyone else will be as trusting or forgiving."

"So what really happened?"

She told Chandra the story, and then sadly shook her head. "I can't believe I was so gullible. I should've seen where Kyle was trying to take things. I feel like such a fool."

Chandra sent her a sympathetic smile. "You wanted to help him. That makes sense."

She huffed. "Too bad Cam doesn't agree."

"What do you mean?"

"I told him everything, but he doesn't believe me."

"Maybe he just needs some time to think it over. I bet he'll come around."

"I don't think so. Once trust is broken, it's hard to repair."

Chandra patted Rachel's back. "I'm sorry. I know you really like him."

She nodded. "I thought he cared about me, too." She shook off that bittersweet thought. "Saving N.C.Y.T. is what matters now. The kids need this program."

"They sure do."

"We can't let the parents shut it down."

"You're absolutely right."

"So I've made my decision."

Chandra blinked. "What do you mean?"

"I'll meet with the parents tomorrow night and answer their questions. If that works, great. If not, I'll step down."

Chandra gasped. "You can't do that! Who'll direct the show?"

Rachel focused on her friend. "You will."

"Whoa, wait a minute. I can't do that. I'm just the choreographer. You're the one who holds everything together."

Those words struck a chord in Rachel's heart, and she shook her head. "No, I'm not. He is," she said, pointing up.

Chandra released a deep breath. "Okay. I see what you mean. But we need to do everything we can to convince those parents you should stay on as director." She bit her lower lip for a few seconds. "I know.

Maybe we could get a few people to speak up for you. I'm sure Suzanne would, and I could, too."

"That's sweet of you to offer, but if things don't go as we hope, then we want them to accept you as my replacement, so you probably shouldn't be too outspoken."

"Okay, but I don't think I'll be able to keep quiet, if they start giving you a hard time."

"We have to put the kids first and save N.C.Y.T." Rachel gripped Chandra's hand. "Promise me you'll remember that, no matter what happens."

"Okay. I promise." Chandra squeezed her hand in return. "I think we need to pray."

"Good idea." Rachel forced optimism into her voice even though she didn't feel it. As she bowed her head, memories of all the tearful prayers she'd prayed in Seattle rushed back. There had been no miracle that time. The answer had been the loss of her job, the scorn of her fellow teachers and friends, and terrible self-doubt. Was she headed for a second round of the same kind of losses?

Her heart ached at that thought, and she forced herself to listen to Chandra's hope-filled words. Finally Chandra finished and waited quietly.

Rachel released a deep breath. "Oh, God, we need a miracle, not just for me, but for my kids. Please save N.C.Y.T. If that means I need to step down, I'm willing. But if You could somehow be my help and defender, I would be so grateful. I love You, and I want to trust You. Help me believe You are working even though I can't see it right now." Then she added a silent P.S. *And could You please help Cam understand and forgive me?* "Amen."

Cam trudged through the back gate and headed for the house. He had hoped to talk to Rachel as soon as he got home from Ross's, but her car was not in the driveway, and she was not answering his calls. Had she turned off her phone, or had she seen his name in the caller ID and refused to answer?

He stomped up the steps. How could he straighten things out if she wouldn't speak to him? Of course he didn't blame her. He'd hurt her with his questions and doubts. He knew that now, but he wasn't sure how he was going to make things right if she didn't come home or answer her phone.

He pushed open the back door and glanced at the clock on the microwave. It was past dinnertime. He wasn't hungry, but he still needed to fix something for Kayla. She'd caught a ride home with Lindsey's mom, while he'd hightailed it over to see Ross.

Closing his eyes, he leaned against the counter and released a heavy sigh. Knowing he'd hurt Rachel bore down on him like a terrible weight, but he had to put that aside for now and focus on Kayla. She'd want to talk it all over. But how could he help his niece when he wasn't doing too well figuring things out for himself? *You'll have to help me with this, Lord, because I don't—*

"Uncle Cam, is that you?" Kayla called.

His eyes flew open. "Yeah, it's me."

She rushed into the kitchen carrying her open laptop. "You've got to read this."

"What is it?"

"Another article about Rachel."

His stomach clenched, and he held up his hand. "No, I don't want—"

"You have to! This one proves she didn't do it."

"What? Let me see."

"I knew she wouldn't do something creepy like that." Kayla passed him the computer and hovered close by.

Cam set the computer on the counter and quickly scanned the article. Only one paragraph long, it reported the charges against Rachel had been dropped and the school board would meet to determine if she would be reinstated as a drama teacher. Every fact matched what Rachel had told him earlier that day. He checked the date and saw it was published three months after the first article he'd read.

He clenched his jaw and swallowed. Three months forced leave of absence, a degrading investigation by police and school officials, terrible lies and rumors, desertion by her friends, and then a scary stalking by the same troubled boy who'd started the whole thing. No wonder she'd wanted to move away and try to forget what happened.

Why hadn't he seen how hard this must have been for her?

"That should convince those parents Rachel didn't do anything wrong." Hope filled Kayla's voice.

"It doesn't really say why the charges were dropped."

"But that means she didn't do it, right?"

Cam laid his hand on Kayla's shoulder. "Rachel says the student lied, then he changed his story several times."

"I knew it! That crazy kid made up the whole thing. Mrs. Mitchell will have to let Haley be in the show now."

"Hold on, sweetie. I know you believe Rachel didn't do anything wrong, but I'm not sure this is enough to make the parents change their minds."

"But that boy lied!"

He held up his hand. "I know."

"So we've got to convince them she's telling the truth!"

Cam rubbed his jaw. Kayla was right. Somehow, they had to prove Rachel was innocent and turn those parents from accusers to supporters, but how could he do that?

Rachel paused on the front steps of the Arts Center and looked up at the beautiful old brick facade, the tall white columns and Palladian windows over the double doors. This had become a wonderful home for N.C.Y.T. Would this be the last time she entered the building as director? Would there even be an N.C.Y.T. after tonight's meeting?

Suzanne tucked her arm through Rachel's. "Ready to go in?"

She straightened her shoulders. "Yes, but I feel a little like Daniel walking into the lion's den."

"Just keep your head up and tell them your story as honestly as you told me and Josh. Everything will be fine."

Rachel sent Suzanne a trembling smile, glad she'd decided to spend the last twenty-four hours with her friend rather than rattling around her empty apartment. "Thanks for coming with me tonight. I really appreciate it."

"Of course. What kind of friend would I be if I sent you in there all by yourself? I just wish I'd seen this coming so I could've tried to defuse the problem earlier."

"You and me both."

"Well, I intend to speak up for you tonight."

"Thanks." If only Cam was as supportive as Suzanne. She pushed that painful thought aside. Now was not the time to mourn the deepening gap in her friendship with Cam. She had to focus on resolving these issues with the parents and saving N.C.Y.T.

She pulled opened the front door, and Hannah

Bodine hurried toward them wearing a determined expression on her face. "We need to pray before you go into that meeting."

Rachel glanced at her watch. "It's already six forty-five. I have to bring up the house lights and be there to meet everyone."

Chandra approached from the other side of the hallway. "I'll get the lights."

"And I'll take care of the lions...I mean...parents." Suzanne winked at Rachel and patted her arm. "You go ahead and pray with your friend. Chandra and I will hold down the fort until you're ready."

Rachel nodded, and Hannah ushered her down the hall and into the little town museum, which was housed on the wing opposite Cam's frame shop and the other artists' galleries.

Rachel glanced at the photos from Fairhaven's earlier days—loggers and seamen, frontiersmen and settlers, all working together to build a new life for themselves and their families. They had come here seeking a fresh start, looking for a place to call home. She carried those same dreams in her heart.

If only she could hold on to them and see them come true here in Fairhaven.

"My daughter told me what's going on," Hannah said, taking her hand. "And I want you to know I'm behind you one hundred percent."

"Thank you, Hannah." Rachel squeezed Hannah's fingers.

"God knows what's happening. He'll take care of it."

Rachel nodded, but her stomach quivered. So much would be decided tonight. If she couldn't persuade the parents to let her continue as director, she'd have to step down, but she wasn't sure how her heart could survive another blow like that.

"Let's pray." Hannah bowed her head. "Lord, we know You desire the truth to come to light tonight. Please give Rachel the strength and confidence she needs to say what You've put in her heart. Help us trust You to work this out in the way that's best for Rachel and the children. Thank You for always hearing our prayers and answering them according to Your will and purpose. In the mighty name of Jesus, Amen."

"Amen." Rachel looked up and forced a small smile for Hannah's sake, but she still felt anxious.

"Okay. Let's go, and remember, I'll be out there praying the whole time."

Ten minutes later Rachel stood at the podium facing sixty or so parents gathered in the first few rows of the auditorium. Haley's mother, Gail Mitchell, sat front and center, flanked by her somber, football-player-sized husband on her right and a few other parents from the first meeting on her left.

Rachel scanned the sea of faces, searching for Cam, but she didn't find him there. Disappointment tugged at her heart. Why had she held on to the foolish hope he would show up and support her? She released a deep breath and let it go. It was time to face her accusers and put her trust in the Lord. He would be her advocate.

"Thank you all for coming. I appreciate the opportunity to meet with you. My goal tonight is to clear up the misunderstandings surrounding what happened to me last year in Seattle. Hopefully, we can resolve these issues and get drama camp and play rehearsals back on schedule so your children can enjoy all the benefits our program has to offer."

She glanced down at her notes. "As I'm sure you've all heard, I left my position as drama teacher at Roosevelt High School because a student accused me of being involved with him in an inappropriate relationship." She looked up and made eye contact with Gail Mitchell. "Those accusations are false, but because of the extended investigation and the doubts that were put in some people's minds, I resigned from my teaching position."

"So you weren't fired from your job?" one of the men in the back of the group called out.

Rattled by the interruption, Rachel gripped the podium. "No, I was not fired. I chose to resign, because I felt that was best for my students and myself."

A low murmur traveled through the group.

"When I came to Fairhaven last January," she continued, "I told Suzanne, our former director, the basic facts about the situation. She has known me for a number of years and she trusted me. She felt what happened in Seattle shouldn't stop me from becoming the new director of N.CY.T." She glanced at Suzanne in the second row, and her friend sent her an encouraging nod.

"But what I failed to tell her was the way my actions contributed to the problem. That was wrong, and I'm sorry for that."

Several of the parents exchanged worried glances.

Rachel pressed on. "Roosevelt has a clear policy about teacher-student relationships. We were instructed to maintain professional boundaries and avoid developing personal relationships. We were also cautioned against engaging in personal communication, meeting with students outside of school or having any kind of physical contact with our students."

Another murmur passed through the crowd.

Rachel clutched her notes. "I crossed some of those boundaries to try to help a troubled student, and he misunderstood my intentions. The problem snowballed, and in the end I had to resign." She glanced around the group, trying to gauge their reactions. Had she told them enough to gain their understanding and support?

Haley's father cleared his throat. "I think we need to know which parts of that policy you broke."

Rachel blew out a deep breath, praying for the right words. There was a very delicate line between protecting Kyle's privacy and giving an honest answer.

"I tried to be a caring friend, but the student interpreted that as romantic interest. Of course, I didn't realize that until it was too late. One day, things reached a crisis. He was very upset, but there was no time to talk at school. So I agreed to meet him off campus. I wanted to convince him to get professional help. That was a worthy goal, but I went about it in the wrong way. I never should've crossed that line or broken the school's policy."

Several parents leaned toward their mates or friends and whispered comments, their faces reflecting doubt and concern. Suzanne chewed her lip, and Hannah closed her eyes and bowed her head.

Rachel released a shuddering breath. Had she just sealed her fate? Was it a lost cause? Should she step down now so Chandra could take over and try to keep N.C.Y.T. going?

Gail Mitchell rose to her feet, her face a steely mask. "Your lack of common sense and disregard for your school's policy make me doubt you have the character or qualifications needed to lead N.C.Y.T." Gail turned toward the parents. "How can we entrust our children to someone who has such poor judgment? Someone who would go behind the back of those in authority over her?"

Rachel's legs weakened. She gripped the podium, wishing she could melt into the floor and disappear.

It was one thing to know the parents were talking about her, it was entirely another to stand there and listen to the hateful words coming out of that woman's mouth.

"I don't know about the rest of you," Gail continued, "but I don't want my daughter exposed to the negative influence of someone—"

The doors of the auditorium burst open, and Cam strode in leading a group of a dozen or more N.C.Y.T. students. The parents all turned to watch them march down the aisle. Rachel locked gazes with Cam. Her heart did a crazy leap in her chest as he strode to meet her at the podium.

The students filed into the front two rows on the right, but her gaze remained trained on Cam.

His eyes radiated warmth and confidence. "Sorry I'm late," he said in a low voice.

"What's going on?" Haley's mother demanded. "We don't want the children in this meeting."

Ryan stood and faced the parents. "We *are* N.C.Y.T., and we're here to support Ms. Clark." The students all clapped.

A swirl of comments from the parents filled the air, some in support of the students staying and others against it.

Cam held up his hand. "I think we can resolve all these issues if everyone will settle down for just a few minutes." He focused on Gail Mitchell and waited. She finally took a seat, and the other parents quieted down.

"My name is Cameron McKenna. I own McKenna's Frame Shop here in the Arts Center, and I'm also the guardian of my niece, Kayla Norton, who is a member of N.C.Y.T. She's been deeply impacted by her involvement in the group, and I've seen how valuable this program is, not just for my niece, but for our whole community. I believe we need to support what's happening here with N.C.Y.T., and we need to realize its success is largely due to the excellent leadership of Rachel Clark."

Rachel's throat grew thick, and she had to blink away her tears. No words of praise had ever sounded sweeter.

"I know there have been a lot of rumors circulating about Ms. Clark," Cam continued, "and I want to put those to rest tonight by introducing a former student of Ms. Clark's from Seattle." He looked to the right and motioned toward the student section.

Rachel followed his gaze and gasped. She'd been so focused on Cam she hadn't seen Kyle Saunders come in with the other students.

Kyle got up and walked toward the podium, his shoulders slumped and his hands stuffed in his jeans pockets. He tossed his head, flicking his long dark hair out of his eyes. His gaze connected with Rachel's for only a split second, but it was long enough for her to see the regret pooled there.

Kyle approached the microphone. He and Cam exchanged a brief look. Cam nodded to Kyle, then guided Rachel to a seat at the end of the first row.

"Are you sure about this?" Rachel asked in a choked whisper.

"Very sure." He settled into the chair next to her.

Kyle shifted from one foot to the other and cleared his throat. Finally, he looked up. "My name's Kyle Saunders. I graduated from Roosevelt High last June. Ms. Clark was my drama teacher my junior year and the first few months of my senior year. She was a good teacher, the best I've ever had." He stopped and looked down, obviously struggling to control his emotions.

"She really cared about me…and all the kids. She tried to help us see what's important in life and teach us how to make good choices." He looked down again and was silent for a few seconds. "That's why I'm really sorry for the things I said about her."

A hushed gasp rose from the group.

Kyle tossed his hair out of his eyes. "I got kind of messed up when my parents divorced a couple years ago. It was pretty rough for a while, and I used to talk to Ms. Clark about it. She always made time to listen to me. She tried to help me think about the future and the good things that could happen if I'd just hang on and not give up or do something stupid to ruin my life. I wasn't a very good listener back then, but that's no excuse for what I did to Ms. Clark." He stopped again for few seconds, fighting to keep his emotions under control. "She never did anything wrong. I was the one that tried to make it into something more, and I'm sorry about that."

Kyle sent Cam a pleading look, as though asking permission to sit down. Cam nodded, and Kyle took a step away from the podium.

"So you're saying you lied. There was no romantic relationship between you and Ms. Clark?" Gail Mitchell's harsh tone carried a heavy dose of accusation.

Kyle blinked, and his Adam's apple bobbed in his throat. "Yeah. I was scared of getting in trouble, so I lied."

Rachel's heart twisted. She felt no surge of triumph over her vindication. Sin had done so much damage in Kyle's life. Her anger and fear melted into sorrow, and the first wave of true forgiveness crested over her heart.

"Could that woman make this any more difficult for him?" Cam muttered, then rose and walked toward the podium.

He placed his hand on Kyle's shoulder. "Thanks, Kyle. We appreciate the courage it took for you to come here and talk to us."

The students clapped for him, and some of the parents joined in. Kyle ducked his head and returned to his seat in the row behind Rachel.

Suzanne got up and joined Cam at the podium. "Thank you, Kyle. It shows real maturity to admit your mistakes and try to make them right. We appreciate that. And I agree with you, Rachel Clark is a wonderful teacher and also an excellent director for N.C.Y.T." She shifted her focus to the parents. "I think it's time to put this issue to rest and give Ms. Clark the assurance of our support. All those in favor of Rachel Clark remaining director of N.C.Y.T. please stand." She stepped forward and beamed a smile at Rachel.

The students jumped up, clapping, hooting and whistling. The parents soon joined in with a hearty round of applause, relief and smiles lighting up their faces.

Tears flooded Rachel's eyes again. She released a shuddering breath and smiled at Cam. He walked toward her. She stood and stepped into his open arms. Relief rushed through her as he held her close for a few seconds and then let her go.

The students surrounded them, showering her with encouraging words. "We love you, Ms. Clark." "You're the best." "We couldn't go on without you."

Kayla stepped forward and hugged Rachel. "Oh, I was praying so hard."

"Me, too." Rachel laughed and swiped a tear from her eye.

Haley joined Kayla. "I'm sorry about my mom. She can be a little overprotective sometimes."

"She loves you, and I'm sure she was just trying to watch out for you."

"Thanks for hanging in there through all of this," Haley added.

The circle of students parted for Haley's parents.

Gary Mitchell cleared his throat. "Ms. Clark, I believe we owe you an apology." He turned to his wife.

Gail nodded, her face flushed. "I'm afraid I jumped to the wrong conclusion. I'm sorry." She hesitated and glanced at her daughter. "I hope Haley can still be in the show."

Rachel smiled and nodded. "There's no one else I'd rather see play Anne."

Several girls squealed and joined Haley and Kayla in a group hug.

Ryan patted Rachel on the back. "Thanks, Ms. Clark. I know we missed a couple rehearsals, but we won't let you down. We'll work hard to get ready."

"Good. Rehearsal is set for tomorrow at one o'clock."

The students cheered, then happily gathered up their belongings and prepared to leave.

Cam placed his arm around her shoulder. "I think there's one more person who wants to talk to you." Cam nodded toward the side of the auditorium where Kyle stood by himself, his eyes downcast.

Rachel's stomach tensed. Was she ready to face Kyle one-on-one? Thinking of all he had been through, her heart went out to him. She glanced up at Cam. "I'll be right back." She crossed the auditorium and walked up the aisle.

Kyle slowly lifted his head. His hair shifted, revealing his somber expression. "I'm sorry for all the trouble I caused you. I never thought you'd lose your job and have to leave. I hope you'll forgive me."

She prayed for the right words. "Everyone makes mistakes and does things they regret. I know I have. But I also know how great it feels to be forgiven. That's what Jesus has done for me." She gently touched his arm and waited until he looked her in the eyes. "I forgive you, Kyle."

His eyes glistened. "Thanks," he said in a hoarse whisper. "I meant what I said about you being the best teacher I ever had."

Rachel's heart brimmed over. "That's a compliment I'll always treasure."

A hint of a smile touched his lips, then he turned and walked up the aisle.

Cam joined her. "Looks like that went well."

Rachel nodded and looked up at him. "How did you ever find Kyle? His name was never in the paper."

Cam chuckled. "Kayla and I drove down to Seattle last night, then first thing this morning we headed over to Roosevelt High. Not too many people work there in the summer, but we found a secretary in the office who was willing to help."

Rachel gasped. "Roberta Kauffman?"

"That's right. She was obviously on your side. She couldn't give us his name or contact info, but she pulled up his record. Then she took a break and mentioned no one would know if we copied the info down while she was out of the room." Cam grinned and rubbed his jaw. "I called his mom, and she invited us over.

"He's been seeing a counselor for the last several months and making good progress. The counselor encouraged him to be ready to apologize to you, if he ever had the chance. So, when I asked him to come to the meeting, he agreed. I won't say he was eager to do it, but he was willing, and that's what counts."

Rachel's heart lifted. "I can't believe you went all the way down there and searched for him."

Cam pulled back, looking surprised. "Well, I had to do something to make up for the way I acted yesterday." He touched her cheek. "I'm sorry. I should've given you the benefit of the doubt instead of being so hardheaded."

Warmed by his touch and apology, she smiled. "And I'm sorry I didn't tell you everything sooner."

He reached for her hand. "This has made me

realize the importance of honesty and openness between us. And there's something I've been wanting to tell you."

"What is it?"

"I've been meeting with Sheldon, talking to him about the accident and what happened to Marie and Tyler." He pulled in a deep breath. "Even though they've been gone almost five years, I've been stuck in the grief process because I felt responsible for what happened."

"But a drunk driver killed your wife and son."

"He's the one who hit us, but I'm the one who put Marie in the driver's seat that night. I should've driven. Maybe then I could've swerved out of the way, or at least turned the car so I could've taken the force of the impact instead of Tyler and Marie."

He bowed his head, sorrow lining his face. "But I was too self-absorbed to see the danger coming and save my family."

"Oh, Cam. It's not your fault."

"That's what Sheldon said."

"Well, he's right. You're not God. You don't know if you could've changed anything that happened even if you were driving." She laid her hand on his cheek. "I'm sorry you lost your wife and son, and I'm so sorry you've carried that burden by yourself all this time, but I'm glad He rescued you from that accident."

He pulled her hand to his lips and kissed her palm.

"Thank you." They embraced and held each other close for a few seconds. "I've got to go. I promised Kyle's mom I'd bring him back tonight."

"You have to drive all the way to Seattle?"

"Yeah. Kayla and I'll stay over at her house. Then we'll drive back in the morning."

"She'll be here for rehearsal, right?"

"Definitely." He kissed her cheek. "Sorry I have to go."

"Me, too."

He pulled her close for one more hug, then turned and jogged up the aisle.

Rachel touched her cheek and smiled. *Thank You, Lord. Thank You, so much!*

Rachel checked her mailbox, pulled out the day's delivery, and unlocked her front door. The sunset's golden beams streamed through the stained-glass window as she climbed the stairs to her apartment. It had been an exhausting day, but N.C.Y.T. had survived, and she and Cam had reconnected.

Her thoughts drifted back to the meeting and all that had happened earlier that evening. It still amazed her to think of the way Kyle's wrong choices and lies had caused so much damage and hurt so many people. But his honest confession had started a chain reaction of good overcoming evil and reconciled a lot of people.

What if she had been unwilling to forgive Kyle?

What if she'd decided to hold on to her right to be angry with him for all he'd done to her? That would've hindered God's plan to protect N.C.Y.T. and reunite her and Cam.

Her decision to forgive Kyle had freed them all.

She laid her purse on the kitchen table and pondered the awesome power of forgiveness. What a great lesson this had turned out to be for her and her students. They would be talking about this for a long time, and she would have plenty of opportunities to help them process what happened and see God's hand in it all.

She closed her eyes and whispered a prayer, thanking God for preparing her heart so she could meet Kyle halfway in the forgiveness process.

Opening her eyes, she glanced across the kitchen table. A shaft of sunlight fell on the letter she had received from her father a few days earlier.

Her heart began to pound. Her father's sinful choices had caused much greater pain than anything Kyle had ever done. But, like Kyle, he had admitted his mistakes and asked forgiveness. And he'd gone even further—searching for her, humbling himself through his confession and asking for a chance to reconnect after all these years.

Rachel pulled his letter from the envelope and ran a trembling finger over the page. Tears blurred her vision as she read his words once more.

How could she withhold forgiveness when she had been forgiven for so much?

But what if he wasn't the man he appeared to be in this letter? What if he let her down and hurt her again? How could she live through that?

She pulled in a deep breath and blew it out slowly.

God had given her the courage and strength to face those parents today and tell the truth. He had also helped her extend His love and forgiveness to Kyle, surely He would take her hand and lead her each step of the way, if she decided to contact her father and rebuild a relationship with him. God was certainly big enough to handle that job, if only she would trust Him.

She gazed out the window at the fading colors of the sunset. "Should I call him? Is that what You're saying?"

A strong sense of assurance filled her heart. She pulled her cell phone from her purse and smoothed out the letter on the table. With another whispered prayer on her lips, she typed in his number.

Chapter Twenty

Rachel glanced at her watch. Only five minutes remained until the curtain would rise for the final performance of N.C.Y.T.'s summer musical. "Okay, everyone, this is it. Let's huddle up." She clasped hands with Kayla on one side and Haley on the other. All the student actors quickly joined them, making a huge circle in the backstage classroom.

Rachel scanned their faces, and her heart felt like it would burst. They had accomplished so much in the last few weeks. Not only had they all pulled together and done an excellent job on the first four performances, they'd all agreed to give up their Labor Day weekend plans to fit in an extra benefit show to help raise funds toward the purchase of the Arts Center.

Chandra rushed into the room waving a piece of paper. "I have a preliminary count on ticket sales." Her bright smile announced the good news before she read it aloud. "We sold 332 tickets at $35 each for a total of $11,620. Plus some people gave extra gifts, so that should bring us over our $12,000 goal!"

The students cheered, and some hooted and slapped each other on the back.

Rachel lifted her hand to quiet them. "Okay, everyone, settle down. We don't want the audience to think there's a fire back here."

"We know the drill," Ryan announced. "Keep a lid on it!"

Everyone laughed, remembering Rachel's constant reminders to keep quiet in the hallways. But tonight she didn't blame them for creating a ruckus. She felt like shouting, too.

Over the last three weeks, she and Cam had grown even closer as he pitched in to finish work on the backdrops and sets, made runs for fast food, and helped out wherever she needed him during the final rehearsals. Then, a little over a week ago, they'd received word that Shannon's treatments were going so well, she and Eric were coming home September 1. Kayla was flying high from that good news.

Rachel's throat tightened as she looked at her students. "I am so proud of every one of you. I'm sure this is N.C.Y.T.'s best show ever. Let's take a minute to thank the Lord."

She bowed her head, and several students spoke short prayers of thanks. She swallowed hard and added her amen, then squeezed Kayla's hand. The squeeze traveled around the circle and back to her. "All right, go out there and give it your very best!"

With radiant smiles on their faces, the students scattered to their positions on stage and in the wings.

Chandra hooked arms with Rachel. "I can take over back here. Why don't you go claim that seat between your two special guests?"

"Okay, thanks." Rachel gave her friend a quick hug, then headed into the auditorium. As the house lights dimmed, she quickly made her way to her seat.

Cam put his arm around her shoulder. "Everything okay backstage?"

"Yes. They're all ready."

Her father leaned toward her. "Looks like you have a packed house."

Rachel nodded and smiled at him, still amazed that he sat beside her.

She had talked to him several times in the past three weeks. A few days ago he'd surprised her by asking if he could visit over Labor Day weekend. She agreed, and they'd made plans together. Rachel asked Cam to go with her to meet him at the airport. She wanted his moral support, but more important, she wanted her father to meet the man who had such a special place in her heart and life.

When John Harding walked into the baggage claim area, she greeted him with a hug, overflowing tears and laughter. Being in her father's arms after all these years was a gift she could hardly comprehend.

The opening prelude began to play, and she focused on the burgundy curtain.

Her father leaned closer. "I was going to wait until after the show, but maybe this will help you reach that goal." He handed her a folded check.

Rachel opened it, squinted at the amount and gasped. "Dad! This is too much."

"No, I've missed a lot of birthdays, Christmases and graduations over the years. I'd like to do this for you."

She nodded and smiled. "Thank you. That's very generous."

"You're welcome." He grinned. "Maybe it will buy me a permanent seat at all your future performances."

"Of course." She leaned over and kissed his cheek. "You'll always have one, right here, front and center."

He took her hand. "I know a gift like that can't make up for all I've missed, but I want you to know I'd be happy to cover the expenses for a wedding of your dreams."

"Dad!" She laughed, thankful the dim lights hid her flushed face. What would Cam think?

"Oh, no rush on that. I just want you to know the money's there should the need arise." He leaned forward and winked at Cam.

Cam grinned. "Thanks. We'll keep that in mind."

An hour and a half later, following the final curtain call, Rachel stood on stage with her cast, holding a beautiful bouquet of coral roses her students had given her. "Thank you for coming tonight. The work of N.C.Y.T. would not be possible without the encouragement and support of our families and friends." She smiled at the audience, then her gaze settled on Cam.

"I'd also like to thank the members of the Arts Center Cooperative who share space with us here. Cam, would you come up and join me?"

The cast and audience clapped as Cam hustled up the steps and met her at center stage, his blue eyes glowing with warmth and affection.

"We'd like to present you with a check toward the purchase of this building. A very generous donor matched our ticket sales tonight, bringing the total to $24,172."

The audience and cast burst into applause.

"Thank you all so much for your generous support." She beamed a smile at her father before turning back to the audience. "We hope this is the first of many productions Northcoast Christian Youth Theater will be able to bring you from this wonderful facility. And now I'd like to invite all the cast members and their families to join us for a celebration in the community room."

* * *

Conversation and laughter filled the air as the cast and their families gathered to visit and share refreshments following the show. In one corner, Ross set up his computer and was already showing video footage he had shot during that evening's performance. Several of the kids gathered around, laughing and joking with each other as they watched themselves singing and dancing across the screen.

Rachel gripped Cam's hand a little tighter as Haley's parents approached.

"Great job, Ms. Clark." Gary Mitchell lifted his punch cup toward her, his gray eyes twinkling.

"Thank you. I'm really proud of Haley and all the kids."

"Well, they couldn't have done it without you and your staff."

Gail Mitchell nodded, then she took her husband's arm and they headed toward the refreshment table.

Cam grinned. "I'd say you've definitely won over this crowd."

"You think so?" Rachel stepped closer, glad she could share this special celebration with Cam.

Kayla wove through the group, still dressed in her wig and costume. "Rachel, These are my parents, Shannon and Eric Norton." A proud smile lit up her face as she introduced them. "And this is Rachel Clark, our director and Uncle Cam's upstairs neighbor."

Shannon reached to shake Rachel's hand. "It's great to finally meet you. Cam and Kayla have been talking about you nonstop."

"Good to meet you, too. I'm so glad you were able to make it back for tonight's performance. Kayla did a terrific job."

"She's quite a little songbird, isn't she?" Eric put his arm around his daughter, and she smiled up at him. "Being in your program this summer has been a real blessing for Kayla. Thanks for making that possible."

"My pleasure."

Kayla leaned to the left and looked across the room. A smile broke over her face. "Come on. There's someone else I want you to meet." She hooked arms with her parents and took them to the circle of friends watching the video. Kayla introduced Ryan to them. He nodded and smiled at Shannon, then shook hands with Eric.

"Good. It's their watch now," Cam said.

Rachel chuckled.

He grinned at her and walked toward the side door.

"Where are we going?"

"Outside."

"But what will the parents say if we disappear?"

He sent her a sly grin. "I don't think they'll notice, but if they do, they'll probably say, 'Way to go, Cam.'"

She laughed and gave him a playful nudge. "You're terrible."

"No, I just want a little time alone with you."

Her stomach fluttered. "I suppose no one would mind if we step out for a few minutes."

He pushed open the door, and hand in hand they walked across the newly planted sod toward a pretty wrought-iron bench that Paxton's Garden Center had donated and installed last week.

Above the last rays of the fading sunset, a few bright stars twinkled overhead. Rachel pulled in a deep breath and let the peaceful surroundings settle her heart.

They sat on the bench. He scooted closer and placed his arm around her shoulder. "I've been thinking about us a lot lately." All the teasing had disappeared from his voice. "And praying, too."

Her heartbeat sped up. "Get any answers?"

"A few." He turned to her and touched her cheek, his blue-eyed gaze intense. "I love you, Rachel, more than I ever thought possible."

Her heart lifted, and a smile bloomed on her lips. "I love you, too. I have for a long time."

That last statement seemed to catch him by surprise. "I never expected to love anyone again. Not because the love Marie and I shared was so great, but more because I felt like a failure at loving her."

She laid her hand over his heart. "I'm sure she didn't think that, Cam."

"Maybe not, but I've learned some important things since then."

She looked up, thrilled he was sharing on such a deep level.

"I know now how important it is to treasure the one you love, to protect her and cherish her…and that's what I intend to do." He pulled her closer, into the circle of his arms. She laid her head on his chest and listened to the sound of his heart beating strong and sure. Then he lowered his lips to meet hers.

They shared a lingering kiss full of tender hope and sweet promises.

Finally he leaned back, but he was still just a whisper away.

Rachel smiled. "All my life I've been looking for a man I could trust and love, someone I could give my whole heart to."

"So do you think you finally found him?" The teasing glint returned to his eyes.

She nodded and smiled, then kissed him again to make sure he knew her answer.

* * * * *

Dear Reader,

Thanks for traveling with me to Fairhaven, Washington, and spending time with Cam, Rachel, Ross, Chandra, Kayla and all the other characters in *Seeking His Love*. I hope you enjoyed the journey! Fairhaven is a real town, a section of Bellingham, Washington, and many of the locations and businesses I mentioned in the story can be found there. If you ever travel through northwestern Washington, I hope you will stop in and pay our friends in Fairhaven a visit.

The themes of forgiveness, honesty and families being reunited are all dear to my heart, and I hope as Rachel and Cam wrestled with them, you were prompted to think about those issues in your own life, as well.

I believe God placed the desire to seek love in everyone's heart. He does this to draw us to Himself and to motivate us to build relationships with others. God longs to provide that love to you. His arms are always open. He is waiting for you to come to Him, pour out your sorrows and failures and receive His forgiveness and love. Jesus makes that all possible for us. What a wonderful Savior!

I would love to hear from you. You may e-mail me at carrie@carrieturansky.com or visit my Web site, www.carrieturansky.com.

Until next time,
Carrie Turansky

QUESTIONS FOR DISCUSSION

1. Rachel believed moving to a new town would help her leave her problems and mistakes behind. Was that a wise decision? Have you ever tried to distance yourself from problems by moving, changing jobs or leaving a relationship? How did that work for you?

2. Cam thought avoiding relationships with women and children would help him deal with the pain of losing his wife and son. Did that help him as he'd hoped? What are some more healthy ways to work through grief?

3. Rachel saw herself as a positive, cup-half-full type of person. Cam was more practical, cautious and logical. How did that affect the way they looked at events in this story? Would you say you are more like Rachel or Cam?

4. Rachel struggled with the issue of honesty. She didn't tell outright lies, but she withheld information, hoping people would see her in a different light. Was that wrong? What principles or guidelines do you use to determine the difference between truth and lies?

5. Cam struggled with regret for not valuing his family or protecting them at the time of the accident. Have you gotten caught up in work, church or other activities that take too much time away from your family? What are some ways you could show your family that you love and value them?

6. When Kayla first came to Fairhaven, she was upset about the possibility of losing her mother to cancer. How did she act out her fears? What helped her overcome them and deal with the unknown future?

7. After losing his wife and son in the accident, Cam pulled away from his Christian friends and did not attend church. Why did he make that decision? What did Cam finally discover when he returned to church?

8. Rachel didn't have the love, encouragement and protection of her father as she grew up. How did this affect her? What influence did your father have on your life?

9. Even though Rachel longed for her father's love, when she received his letter, she struggled with the decision to contact him. Why was that hard

for her? What helped her make the decision to finally call her father?

10. Gail Mitchell and several other N.C.Y.T. parents jumped to the wrong conclusions about Rachel when they read the online newspaper article about her. Have you ever judged someone from reading an article or hearing gossip about them?

11. Kyle Saunders's false accusations had a huge impact on Rachel and hurt many other people. Have you ever seen the way one person's sin affects many people's lives? How did Kyle's decision to tell the truth affect Rachel's situation?

12. Rachel, Chandra and the students involved in N.C.Y.T. formed a close bond by working together and performing the musical. Have you ever experienced that kind of bond by working closely with others on a project, performance, mission trip or other activity? Did that bond last?

13. How do you see the title tying in to the story? Whose love was Cam seeking and whose did he find? Whose love was Rachel seeking and whose did she find? Who has helped you on your search to find and enjoy more of God's love?

LARGER-PRINT BOOKS!

**GET 2 FREE
LARGER-PRINT NOVELS
PLUS 2 FREE
MYSTERY GIFTS**

Love Inspired®

Larger-print novels are now available...

Love Inspired® SUSPENSE

RIVETING INSPIRATIONAL ROMANCE

Watch for our new series of
edge-of-your-seat suspense novels.
These contemporary tales
of intrigue and romance
feature Christian characters
facing challenges to their faith...
and their lives!

NOW AVAILABLE IN REGULAR & LARGER-PRINT FORMATS

Steeple
Hill®

Visit:
www.SteepleHill.com

Love Inspired.
HISTORICAL

INSPIRATIONAL HISTORICAL ROMANCE

Engaging stories of romance,
adventure and faith,
these novels are set in
various historical periods
from biblical times
to World War II.

NOW AVAILABLE!

Steeple
Hill®